THE MYTHICAL **9th** DIVISION

OPERATION ROBOT STORM

ALEX MILWAY

Kane Miller
A DIVISION OF EDC PUBLISHING

For Cecily, my own little yeti

First American Edition 2012
Kane Miller, A Division of EDC Publishing

Copyright © 2010 Alex Milway

For information contact:
Kane Miller, A Division of EDC Publishing
PO Box 470663
Tulsa, OK 74147-0663
www.kanemiller.com
www.edcpub.com

Library of Congress Control Number: 2011928499

Printed and bound in the United States of America

ISBN: 978-1-61067-074-6

www.mythical9thdivision.com

FOR 150 YEARS A **MYSTERIOUS** TRIO OF HEROIC AND RESOURCEFUL YETIS HAS EXISTED AS A **TOP-SECRET** BRANCH OF THE BRITISH ARMED FORCES. OVER THE YEARS, SUCCESSIVE GENERATIONS OF YETIS HAVE WORKED FEARLESSLY TO DEFEND THE WORLD AGAINST **THE FORCES OF EVIL**. AS THESE POWERS GROW EVER DEADLIER, THE YETIS FIGHT ON, PITTING BOTH **STRENGTH** AND **WITS** AGAINST THE MIGHT OF THEIR ENEMIES.

THEY ARE THE MYTHICAL 9TH DIVISION.

SUMMER TEMPERATURES PLUMMET!

Simon Frost reporting from Snowdonia

The most serious cold snap to threaten the country in a hundred years is causing mayhem in much of North Wales. Last night temperatures dropped further, reaching -22°F over Snowdonia, and the temperature is expected to fall further still.

Forecasters were completely surprised by the drastic change in weather and cannot explain the sudden appearance of a huge storm front over the area. They are predicting blizzards and ice storms over higher ground tonight.

The immediate area has been evacuated, and the authorities are urging those in other parts of the country to travel to friends and family elsewhere.

THE MYTHICAL **9**th DIVISION

Chapter 1: An Unfortunate Interruption

MT. EVEREST. THE TALLEST MOUNTAIN IN THE WORLD. HOME OF THE ANNUAL INTERCONTINENTAL CHALLENGE...

THE USA VERSUS BRITAIN

BIGFOOT VERSUS...

YETI

FZZZZZ

NOT NOW...

ALB...
FZZZZZ

ZZZ...RECHT

I DON'T
BELIEVE
THIS!

FZZZZZ

12

FZZZZZZZ!

NOOOO!!

Albrecht was the leader of the Mythical 9th Division, a secret troop of yetis that worked for the British Army. He was well-built (though not big-boned) and had glossy, golden-brown fur. In fact, you could say he was a pretty good-looking yeti. The other thing you could say about Albrecht was that he never disobeyed an order from his superiors. Never…

"Fzzzz ALBRECHT! COME IN, ALBRECHT! Fzzzz!"

Albrecht slid to a halt and swung his arm around behind his backpack. His fingers unlatched his RoAR, the communications tool that kept him in touch with the army. A stream of diagonal lines shot across its small screen, and he pulled up the aerial to improve reception.

The speaker crackled again.

"FZZZZZZ fzzzzz fzzzz!"

Albrecht banged the RoAR against a rock, and a picture appeared on the screen.

"Captain!" said Albrecht, as the face of Captain James T. Ponkerton filled the small screen. He wore a flat military cap, a bushy moustache and sported a uniform the color of overcooked peas.

"FZZzzzzzz… Are you there?!" said Ponkerton.

"Yes, sir," said Albrecht loudly, struggling to be heard over the whistling wind. "But I'm having problems with the RoAR."

"We're all having problems," said the Captain. "Humanity is facing its greatest test yet. In fact—"

"Test?" interrupted Albrecht. "Like a math exam?"

"More like French grammar," said Ponkerton gravely. "Nothing makes any sense…"

Albrecht heard a noise to his side and turned to see a tall, two-legged hairy beast running towards him. It was bigger than Albrecht – which was no mean feat – but it *was* a bigfoot, after all.

"Hold on a second, Captain," said the yeti.

The bigfoot had huge black goggles and breathing apparatus strapped to his face. His long brown fur trailed behind him like the tail of a comet, and a U.S. flag was secured to the oxygen

THE MYTHICAL **9th** DIVISION

ITEM: RoAR
SERIAL No: 5674-90/YETI
STATUS: *TOP-SECRET*

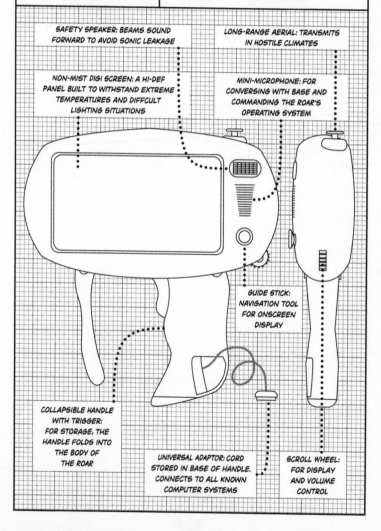

SAFETY SPEAKER: BEAMS SOUND FORWARD TO AVOID SONIC LEAKAGE

LONG-RANGE AERIAL: TRANSMITS IN HOSTILE CLIMATES

NON-MIST DIGI SCREEN: A HI-DEF PANEL BUILT TO WITHSTAND EXTREME TEMPERATURES AND DIFFCULT LIGHTING SITUATIONS

MINI-MICROPHONE: FOR CONVERSING WITH BASE AND COMMANDING THE ROAR'S OPERATING SYSTEM

GUIDE STICK: NAVIGATION TOOL FOR ONSCREEN DISPLAY

COLLAPSIBLE HANDLE WITH TRIGGER: FOR STORAGE, THE HANDLE FOLDS INTO THE BODY OF THE ROAR

UNIVERSAL ADAPTOR: CORD STORED IN BASE OF HANDLE. CONNECTS TO ALL KNOWN COMPUTER SYSTEMS

SCROLL WHEEL: FOR DISPLAY AND VOLUME CONTROL

tank on his back. This was no ordinary bigfoot. This was a bigfoot of the Mythical 6th Division.

"Don't mind if I do!" said the bigfoot, as he powered on past.

Albrecht growled angrily.

"Unfortunately, the Challenge will have to wait," continued Ponkerton, his words forcing the yeti to focus again. "We need your sub-zero experience back home."

"Britain?" said Albrecht.

"Wales is suffering the coldest weather on record."

"And?" said Albrecht.

"It should be summer," said Ponkerton.

"Oh…"

"The fact of the matter is this: Some of our best, Arctic-trained soldiers have gone missing in the mountains of Snowdonia, and we need you to get them back…"

Albrecht's eyes wandered to the mountainside, watching as the bigfoot disappeared through a crack in the rock. The Challenge was lost.

"Albrecht!" The Captain's voice crackled out of the RoAR again.

"Sorry?" said Albrecht, dragging his eyes back to the screen. "You want us to rescue humans?"

"I wouldn't normally ask you, but these are exceptional circumstances," said the Captain, looking deadly serious.

Apart from the Tibetan monks, the Ponkertons were the only human family ever to befriend the yetis and had worked with them since the 1850s when the Mythical 9th Division was first created. Captain Ponkerton had commanded the division for over 30 years, and in all that time he had made sure the yetis' existence was kept secret from the human population.

But now the Captain's orders were clear.

"Assemble the team and rescue our boys," he said.

Albrecht couldn't believe what he was hearing.

"With respect, sir, we don't do humans…"

"I know, but just this once I'm asking you to break that rule. Our soldiers discovered something in Snowdonia. Unfortunately they lost signal before we could find out what. If they found the origins of this deadly, unseasonal weather, then we need them back. You're the only ones who can do it."

Albrecht felt his sense of duty take over.

"Yes, sir," he said. "I'd better find the others. How long do I have?"

"You've got 24 hours before Sherpa I takes you to Wales. Time is of the essence. We need to know what those soldiers found – the people of Snowdonia can't hold out much longer."

Albrecht took a deep breath and saluted.

"We'll find your soldiers for you, sir," he said.

"Terrific," said Ponkerton, saluting back. "I'll be in touch."

The screen of the RoAR fizzled to black, and Albrecht was left alone on the mountain. It finally sunk in that he'd lost the Challenge. The other members of the Mythical 9th Division were not going to be happy.

Chapter 2: Wrestling with Yaks

"Take your hairy face away from here!" boomed Timonen, his words echoing down the valley.

"Aaargh, Timonen! You need to calm down!" Albrecht pleaded. Being fifty yards below an angry yeti on a mountainside was a precarious position to be in.

Timonen disappeared from view, and a moment later a small blue radio flew down and smashed into pieces at Albrecht's feet.

"Bigfoot radio reported that you stopped to take a call!" roared Timonen, his voice rumbling through the air like thunder. "You had to take a CALL?!"

"It was the Captain!" shouted Albrecht. "I had no choice. You can't not take a call from Captain Ponkerton!"

Without warning, another missile came plummeting down. Albrecht opened his arms wide and squeezed his eyes shut. A second later he was squashed to the floor as an unhappy yak hit

him with full force, its horns barely missing his head. The angry yak scrambled to its feet and galloped off across the ice, grunting to itself.

"Thanks..." coughed Albrecht, struggling for breath.

By now, Timonen was careening down the slope, his hands and feet clawing at the gravel and rocks, pulling him down faster.

"You're lucky it was only one!" he said.

His bronze fur sparkled in the icy conditions, and with a final jump, he landed at the foot of the mountain. He held out a hand to his friend on the ground.

"You're too kind," spluttered Albrecht, as he was pulled upright.

Standing next to Timonen made Albrecht feel small, even human. Timonen was a beefcake: His hands were nearly twice as wide as his friend's, his fur was much longer, and his legs were like tree trunks.

"So we've got a new mission?" said Timonen.

"A rescue mission," said Albrecht, spitting a clump of yak fur from between his teeth.

Timonen's black eyes lit up. He lifted Albrecht into the air and shook him violently.

"A RESCUE MISSION!" he barked excitedly.

"Please put me down," said Albrecht calmly. "My lunch is threatening to reappear."

Timonen planted him back on the ground with such force that his legs were driven ankle-deep into the ground.

"But we never get rescue missions!" said Timonen, clenching his massive fists and hopping from one foot to the other. "Who are we saving? A princess? A film star? A rare-breed yak?"

"No, some British soldiers," said Albrecht, forcibly removing his feet from the ground.

Timonen lost every ounce of enthusiasm.

"Soldiers?" he said. "Can't they look after themselves?"

"Clearly not," said Albrecht. "They're missing in the mountains of Wales."

"Where's that?" asked Timonen, never one to let knowledge get in the way of his mighty strength.

"Britain," said Albrecht. "You work for the British government!"

"Is Wales the one with a yak on its flag?" he replied.

"Dragon," said Albrecht. "They have a dragon. I don't think there *are* any national flags with yaks."

"Shame," said Timonen.

"It is," said Albrecht. "Now if you're happy with all this, we need to find Saar."

Timonen rolled his eyes.

"Why do we always have to take the mystic with us?" he whined.

Albrecht walked off, shaking his head.

"There are three of us," he called back over his shoulder. "We're a team. We need him."

Timonen shrugged.

"But he wears a *scarf*," he said. "I'm embarrassed to be seen with him."

"He's older than you," said Albrecht. "He needs it to keep warm, and you should respect that."

Timonen clapped his heavy hand on Albrecht's backpack.

"Whatever you say, boss."

THE MYTHICAL 9th DIVISION

Chapter 3: The Third Yeti

THE RONGLAN MONASTERY, TIBET

IF YOU CAN'T WALK QUIETLY, YOU'LL HAVE TO WAIT HERE.

FINE, I'M OFF...

SOMEONE HAS TO BE IN CHARGE OF FOOD.

HEY!

COME BACK!

Saar was by far the oldest of the three yetis, and where Timonen had strength and Albrecht had agility, he had wisdom.

"So you lost," said Saar, his voice calm and collected.

"You've heard already?" said Albrecht.

"The wind passes through the monastery just like it does the mountains."

"The wind?" said Albrecht. "The wind tells you things?"

Saar laughed his deep, languid laugh.

"We have radios here too, Albrecht," he said, turning around. "But since I know you wouldn't let us down for a mere phone call, I'm guessing it was Captain Ponkerton with a new mission."

"Bingo," said Albrecht.

Saar stood up and shook out his legs. He wrapped a thin striped scarf around his neck, flicked it over his shoulder and picked up his long wooden staff – the magical Staff of Ages that had been passed down through yeti hands for thousands of years.

"I'm ready," he said, running his fingers through the fur on his head.

"You'd better prepare yourself," said Albrecht quickly. "This is no ordinary mission."

Saar raised an eyebrow.

"Really?"

"It's a *rescue* mission – humans."

"Humans?" said Saar. "Is Ponkerton sure about this?"

"Orders are orders."

"But humans and yetis don't mix, Albrecht…"

"Look, everything will be fine," he replied. "It's a simple mission."

Saar's fingers gripped his staff even tighter.

"Nothing is simple when Timonen's involved."

"Oh, please," said Albrecht. "We're a team, you know that!"

Saar walked to a golden Buddha sitting against the wall and rested his thin fingers on its head.

"Timonen has nothing but fur for brains," he said, twisting the Buddha to face the opposite direction.

The wall slid sideways to reveal a secret passage.

"However," he added sagely, "I cannot deny that his strength sometimes comes in handy. Let's go."

"Erm, couldn't we just leave through the door?" asked Albrecht.

Saar rolled his eyes. "This is supposed to be a *secret* rescue mission…"

They walked into the passage, and the wall slid back into place behind them, covering their path. Albrecht touched the walls, tracing the lines of drawings made by the ancient yetis. They looked as old as the monastery itself.

"The Staff of Ages is unsettled tonight," said Saar conversationally. "It would appear there's trouble brewing."

"It's probably just Timonen," said Albrecht. "He went to get food for the journey, and you know what that means."

"No one in Tibet will eat for the next week?" Saar replied.

The passage grew narrower as they progressed, and eventually the drawings were replaced by damp stone walls. A few more steps took them out into the crisp starlit night.

*　*　*

"Timonen!" called Albrecht.

The big yeti was sitting on a rock next to the pickup zone. A huge slab of dried meat dangled from his giant hands, and a sack of lentils lay behind him.

"Evening," he muttered, tearing a lump out of the meat with his teeth.

Albrecht pressed a button on the side of his backpack, and a small, pencil-like device dropped into his fingers. It was a Sonic Flare, an electronic fire-lighter that could spark a fire in even the wettest conditions. The yeti grabbed some dried scrub from the surrounding area and proceeded to set fire to it.

"What a surprise to find you eating," said Saar, sitting down next to Albrecht, the ball of fire now blazing on the floor.

"Want some?" said Timonen.

Saar shook his head.

"You know I'm a vegetarian," he said. "Besides, I've already eaten."

"Isn't it nice to be back together again?" said Albrecht wearily, placing more brush and wood onto the fire.

The other yetis didn't respond. Timonen plonked the meat down on the ground and began to warm his hands in front of the flames. As Albrecht sat staring at the deep black sky, his backpack started to vibrate. It was his RoAR again.

"Albrecht," said the voice of Captain Ponkerton. "Come in, Albrecht!"

The yeti unlatched the device and held it up to see the screen.

"Sherpa I is on its way," said the Captain. "I should warn you that conditions are worsening over Wales. Our satellite imagery is now totally obscured by this blasted storm over Snowdonia. Looks like you'll be on your own once this mission's under-way."

THE MYTHICAL **9th** DIVISION

ITEM: SHERPA 1
SERIAL No: 5673-81/YETI
STATUS: *TOP-SECRET*

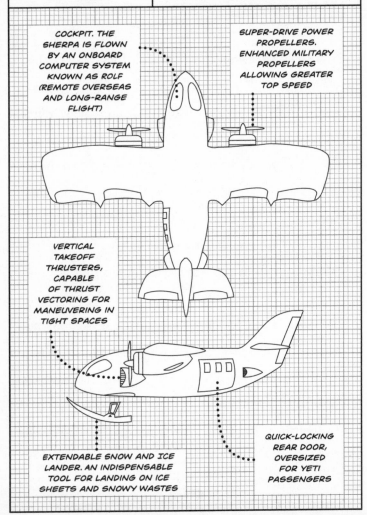

COCKPIT. THE SHERPA IS FLOWN BY AN ONBOARD COMPUTER SYSTEM KNOWN AS ROLF (REMOTE OVERSEAS AND LONG-RANGE FLIGHT)

SUPER-DRIVE POWER PROPELLERS. ENHANCED MILITARY PROPELLERS ALLOWING GREATER TOP SPEED

VERTICAL TAKEOFF THRUSTERS, CAPABLE OF THRUST VECTORING FOR MANEUVERING IN TIGHT SPACES

EXTENDABLE SNOW AND ICE LANDER. AN INDISPENSABLE TOOL FOR LANDING ON ICE SHEETS AND SNOWY WASTES

QUICK-LOCKING REAR DOOR, OVERSIZED FOR YETI PASSENGERS

"Don't worry about us, sir," said Albrecht. "We can deal with it."

"Good," said Ponkerton. "You'll be dropped at a safe house a short distance from the cold zone. We think that everyone has been evacuated from the area, but you should still be on your guard, just in case."

"Captain," said Saar, "are you sure this is wise? Do you remember what happened the last time we were sighted?"

"Ah, yes – my father told me about the 1953 Everest expedi-tion—"

"I was only a boy!" Timonen interrupted angrily, spitting a wad of chewed meat from his mouth. "Stop blaming me for everything."

"You risked our whole existence to steal a can of corned beef and some trail mix from those climbers!" said Saar. "What do you expect?"

"But they only saw my footprints! It could have been much worse. I might have been having a bath!"

"And that would have been horrible," said Albrecht.

"Now, now," said Ponkerton, who was keen to avoid a fight,

"let's not get into all that again. I've thought a lot about this, and I've come to the conclusion that few people will believe in yeti sightings in the Welsh mountains. Besides, I've sent a map to the RoAR showing the route with the lowest human population density. It'll take you right to where we last heard from our troops."

Suddenly the sound of engines pierced the silence of the mountain.

"OK, boys," said Albrecht. "Get ready for the journey."

"I'll contact you when you land," said Ponkerton. "I should know more of the situation then."

Albrecht saluted and returned the RoAR to his backpack. Three ropes dropped from the sky, and the yetis took hold.

"Ready?" said Albrecht.

Saar growled.

Timonen growled and picked up the sack of lentils with his spare hand.

"Here we go!"

THE MYTHICAL 9th DIVISION

Chapter 4: A Shaky Start

SOMEWHERE ABOVE THE HIMALAYAS

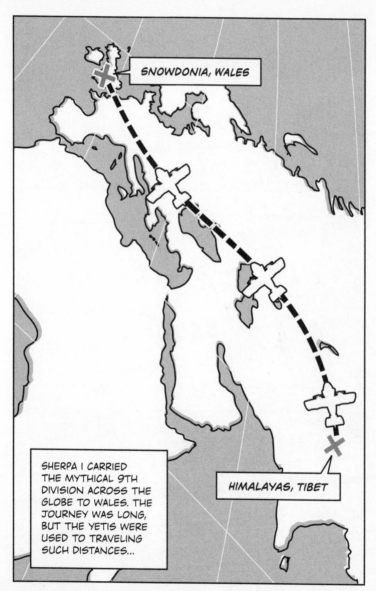

DESTINATION
HOURS:0 MINS:0 SECS:0

A green light flashed on in the hold of Sherpa I. The hatch opened in front of Albrecht, and after a sharp shove in the back, he found himself hurtling through the freezing night air, his arms outstretched and eyes shut tight. The howling wind and rain blasted into his face mask, whipping his fur into ever-changing new hairstyles.

When he finally opened his eyes, he saw the dark, mist-covered Earth flying towards him.

"You're straying from the target," said Saar, his calm voice crackling in Albrecht's earpiece.

Unlike the other two, Saar was soaring like a condor.

"I hate flying," grumbled Albrecht breathlessly, twisting his body a little and righting his descent.

"That's better," said Saar, watching his friend with an amused eye.

Albrecht tugged a cord at his side, and his parachute blew open above him.

"Now, your turn, Timonen," said Saar. "You've done this many times. Take a deep breath and pull the cord."

Through his earpiece, Albrecht heard a growl of a reply – the big yeti always struggled to find the cord through his dense fur. When his fingers eventually caught hold, his parachute opened and sent him drifting way off target.

"Now, straighten up," said Saar.

"I can't go straight!" roared Timonen. "The wind's too strong!"

Albrecht looked over to his right and saw Timonen's massive bulk floating away into the distance like a limp, shaggy rug.

"Think of yourself as a leaf sailing on the breeze," suggested Saar.

"Think of yourself as a pain in the neck!" yelled Timonen.

With the hazy ground rapidly coming closer, Albrecht caught sight of the dull red light of the mountain-top beacon which was their target. It flashed every few seconds, and as he saw it for the second time, he pulled his steering cord to right

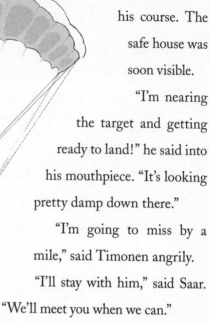

his course. The safe house was soon visible.

"I'm nearing the target and getting ready to land!" he said into his mouthpiece. "It's looking pretty damp down there."

"I'm going to miss by a mile," said Timonen angrily.

"I'll stay with him," said Saar. "We'll meet you when we can."

"See you on the other side!" replied Albrecht, whose eyes were firmly fixed on the fast-approaching ground.

With just feet to go, Albrecht pulled hard at the cords hanging from his side. His feet thudded into the ground, and a thick spray of mud flew up around him. His legs crumpled, he tumbled and rolled and finally came to rest with his face mask wound around his neck. He spat out a handful of dirt and grass that had forced its way into his mouth.

"Hello, ground," he said, detaching the parachute from his backpack.

He cast his eyes over the surrounding landscape, most of which was shrouded in murky cloud and misty rain. There wasn't a light to be seen. The mountain was silent and empty, apart from the safe house, which had seen better days and looked more like a pile of rotten wood than a house.

Albrecht walked closer. The door was barely resting on its hinges, and the slate roof was missing more than a few tiles. The one small window was cracked and covered with cobwebs, and the knotty wood that made up its walls was dotted with mold.

The yeti pushed at the door, which squealed and twisted inwards. Apart from a few puddles of water, the shack's interior was fairly dry. Albrecht shook his fur, sending a spray of droplets around the room. At the press of a button on the side of his backpack, an oval lamp slid from its top and started to glow. By the time Albrecht had set it on the threadbare rug, it was shining at full strength, and the shack was awash with a vibrant blue light.

"Cute place," he said, spying the small wood burner and a rocking chair in the corner.

He walked over to a blurry old photograph hanging on the wall and brushed the dust from its surface. He revealed a man, covered in dirt, who was smiling and holding a lump of black rock in the air.

Suddenly Albrecht's backpack started to vibrate, and with the press of another button, the RoAR slid from its top. The image of Captain Ponkerton on its screen was very faint, so Albrecht tried lifting the aerial, which made no difference at all.

"Captain," said Albrecht, "I've got reception issues again."

"I wasn't sure I'd get you," replied the Captain. His moustache was bristling, and he looked as though he hadn't slept since they last spoke. "So much has happened since you took to the air… I must talk fast, as I fear we may lose contact altogether."

"Go on," said Albrecht.

"Right, yes… The weather … did you notice the weather?"

Albrecht went to speak, but he was halted by a loud *crunch*. It was the sound of the shack's wall being torn off. The cold wind rushed in, and a drenched Timonen stood in the newly created hole, wall held aloft.

"What a poky little—"

"Can't you just use the door?" asked Saar, strolling past and prodding him with his staff.

"As a matter of fact—" began Timonen.

"For goodness' sake!" Albrecht interrupted, before the argument could escalate. "Just put the wall back where you found it."

"Everything all right?" asked the Captain, his voice stuttering through the small speaker on the RoAR.

"The others have arrived, that's all," said Albrecht.

Timonen ducked down to step inside and then tried to put the wall back behind him, but it was a waste of time. In the end he had to prop it up against the roof, but there was still a breeze whipping in through the gaps at either side.

"You were saying?" said Albrecht to the RoAR.

"Ah, yes," said Ponkerton. "Ice. There's ice everywhere."

"I don't follow," said Albrecht.

"The storm over Snowdonia is blurring our satellite imagery, but in the cold zone, the land is freezing over."

"Well, I can assure you it's raining here," said Albrecht.

"That's what we'd expect in Wales at this time of year. But just a short distance down the valley, if our pictures are correct..."

Ponkerton paused for a moment to wipe his brow and continued.

"Well, a glacier is forming. Rivers of ice are growing bigger by the second. Widening, taking over the land."

The yetis looked at each other, not fully understanding Captain Ponkerton.

"You're saying a glacier has sprung up out of nowhere in the space of a few days?" said Albrecht.

"That's exactly what I'm saying. And it's coming directly from the spot where our troops went missing," said Ponkerton. "We've been charting it on our weather maps, and there's no other possibility. It's as if we've been thrown back into the Ice Age overnight."

"That sounds highly unlikely," said Saar.

Ponkerton lifted his army cap and scratched the thinning hair on his head.

"That's because it *is* highly unlikely," he said.

With a fizz and a buzz, the screen suddenly went blank.

"Where's he gone?" said Timonen.

Albrecht hit the RoAR with the palm of his hand, but the screen remained dead.

"Utter rubbish!" he said. He tried pointing the aerial in different directions, but it didn't help.

"So while we're on the subject, let me get one thing straight," said Timonen. "Wales doesn't usually have glaciers?"

"Correct," said Saar. "Wales is warmer than where we're from."

"Right," said Timonen. "But what about the mountains?"

"Smaller," said Albrecht. "Much, much smaller."

He flicked a switch on the RoAR, and the map Ponkerton had sent appeared on the screen.

"At least we have this," he said. "That'll be some help."

"So what now?" said Saar.

"We wait till dawn, then head out," said Albrecht. "We need to get some rest. There's no knowing what we'll find in the wilderness of Wales."

THE MYTHICAL 9th DIVISION

Chapter 5: A Chilly Surprise

"**Y**ou'll want to see this," said Albrecht, hurrying himself back into the wooden shack.

Timonen was picking his toenails and flicking them at Saar. The mystic yeti was used to this and swatted them away with his staff.

"Ponkerton was right."

"A glacier?" said Saar.

"Wider than any in Tibet," said Albrecht. "And there's nothing natural about it."

"We should make a move," said Saar.

Timonen lifted his foot to rip a final piece of nail from his big toe with his teeth. Albrecht watched in horror as the big yeti swallowed it down.

"Ready," said Timonen, standing up so that his head was pressed against the roof. He pushed down the broken wall with the touch of a finger.

"First rule of mountain life," said Saar wearily, "leave your camp as you found it."

"Huh?" sniffed Timonen, as he marched out of the shack and stopped on the grassy slope.

Saar gave Albrecht a tired look.

"I'm not taking any responsibility for him," he said, spiraling his scarf around his neck.

"He knows what's required of him," said Albrecht.

"Does he really?" said Saar.

"Yes, I do," said Timonen.

The yetis stood in a row, looking down the hillside towards the valley and the glacier.

"It's so different from Tibet," said Albrecht.

Timonen crossed his arms.

"And to make things worse," he said, "I haven't seen a yak anywhere."

* * *

The yetis marched down the hillside, clambering over fences and stepping over streams and hedges. It was unfamiliar territory, but Albrecht followed the course marked on the map, and they made good progress. After an hour's walk, they were standing at the base of the glacier. Above them was a vertical climb of at least a hundred yards.

The glacier was growling and grumbling as it moved slowly forward. The yetis felt the temperature dip.

"That's more like it," said Timonen. "A nice bit of cold."

Saar tapped his staff on the ground.

"Still no news from Ponkerton?" he asked.

"Nothing," said Albrecht.

"Then let's get a move on," said Timonen. "I'm not here for the sightseeing!"

Albrecht withdrew three pairs of spiky metal climbing tools from his backpack and passed them to his friends. The yetis slipped their hands through the straps and clutched them tight. Saar tied his staff into the end of his scarf and let it hang by his side, leaving his hands free.

Timonen was the first to act. He jumped high in the air

 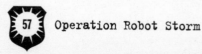

and punched his right fist into the ice, digging the spikes into the smooth surface. He hung there for a moment, then reached up and smashed his left fist higher up. The other yetis did the same, and they were soon making good progress.

The yetis were adept at rock climbing and navigated the sheer ice cliff in double-quick time. They drew themselves up onto its top and caught their breath.

Dark gray clouds were forming overhead, and an aging layer of snow rested on the icy ground.

"We should try to make that hill by nightfall," said Albrecht, pointing to a rocky outcrop in the far distance that still stood out from the ice sheet.

Saar sniffed the air, seemingly smelling the elements.

"The weather's only going to get worse from here on in," he said.

The yetis trekked across the icy plateau, the wind biting through their furry coats. The clouds were gathering above them as though summoned by a Norse god to halt their progress. For the moment though, the snow was holding off. Timonen had

THE MYTHICAL 9th DIVISION

ITEM: YETI CLIMBING
EQUIPMENT
SERIAL No: 5672-72/YETI
STATUS: *TOP-SECRET*

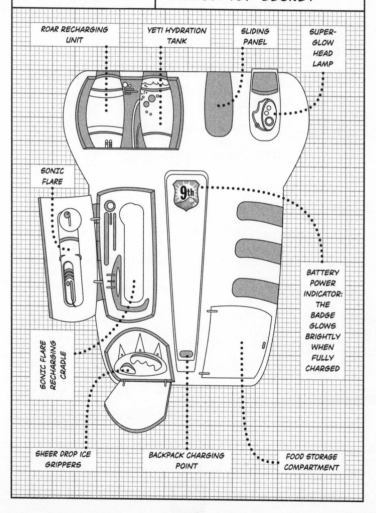

ROAR RECHARGING
UNIT

YETI HYDRATION
TANK

SLIDING
PANEL

SUPER-
GLOW
HEAD
LAMP

SONIC
FLARE

BATTERY
POWER
INDICATOR:
THE
BADGE
GLOWS
BRIGHTLY
WHEN
FULLY
CHARGED

SONIC FLARE RECHARGING CRADLE

SHEER DROP ICE
GRIPPERS

BACKPACK CHARGING
POINT

FOOD STORAGE
COMPARTMENT

taken the lead and was making good headway when he stopped dead in his tracks.

"They *do* have yaks in Wales!" he said excitedly.

Out on the ice in front of him stood a small herd of hairy animals.

"I think you'll find they're sheep," said Saar.

"Sheep?" he replied.

Timonen walked closer and realized that the animals were actually quite short. They barely reached his ankles.

"Baaaaaaaa," bellowed the herd.

"Baby yaks!" exclaimed Timonen.

The sheep had huddled together to keep warm. Their thick brown and white woolly coats darted back and forth in the swirling wind, and their long faces were hidden from view under thick manes of dangling curls.

"It's a totally different species," muttered Saar.

Timonen patted one with his enormous hand.

"They don't look much different," he said. "And they shouldn't be out here on the ice."

Albrecht sighed. He knew what this meant. One by one,

 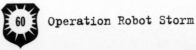

Timonen piled the sheep onto his shoulders.

"What?" said the fully-laden yeti. "Just keeping the place tidy!"

"I'm starting to think that this obsession with yaks is un-healthy," said Albrecht, staring at the towering pyramid of sheep ahead of them.

Saar looked on in disbelief.

"It's a good thing we don't want anyone to see us," he said sarcastically. "There's nothing at all unusual about a tower of sheep… I bet people see them all the time in Wales."

Further and further they marched, and as day turned to evening, the snow began to fall from the skies above them. By the time they reached the base of the mountain, a blizzard was raging. Lumps of snow had settled in their fur, and their eyebrows drooped under the weight of frosty icicles.

Saar stopped to tighten his scarf and realized there was a building ahead of them.

"Is that smoke?" he said.

Where the gray stone of the mountain met the white glacier,

 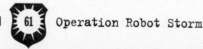

a run-down building lurched perilously above the ice. Attached to its side was a cylindrical, broken chimney. Small clouds of smoke puffed from its crumbling top.

"People?" said Albrecht. "Here?"

"I thought everyone had left," said Saar.

"Something fishy's going on," growled Timonen, lowering the sheep from his shoulders one by one. "Look after this bunch. I'm going to find out what's up."

A few large boulders sat atop the ice sheet, dragged from the hillside by the moving glacier. Using one of these as cover, Timonen slid to a halt and dropped to the ground. He peered around the boulder and saw movement at the base of the building. Suddenly a pair of lights burst out of the gloom and moved as one, circling back and forth across the ground. Timonen turned back to alert his fellow yetis, but they were already at his side. The herd of sheep was grumbling from afar.

"What *is* that?" said Saar.

"It's some sort of snowmobile," said Albrecht, who was staring at the lights through his top-of-the-line electronic binoculars.

"Where'd you get those?" asked Timonen.

"Standard issue," he replied. "If you bothered to carry your own military backpack, you'd know."

Timonen huffed.

"All I need are my fists," he said.

"Hang on," said Saar. "Who's driving that thing?"

Albrecht flicked a switch on his binoculars and zoomed in closer.

"Robots?" he said.

"WHAT!" exclaimed Saar.

Albrecht pressed a button, and the picture came into focus. The robots were made of white metal, with thin bands across their faces that held their glowing blue eyes. They were human-shaped, and they looked angry.

"Definitely robots," he replied. "And they're coming right at us."

A look of pure joy came over Timonen's face. He jumped out of hiding and ran at the two beams of light now heading straight for him. He surged forward with his arms flailing from left to right and his feet tearing at the snow to make him go

faster. The growling engine drew closer, and just as Timonen was about to leap fist-first into the blinding lights, he ground to an abrupt halt and began to run back towards the boulder.

"Lasers!" he roared. "Lasers!"

A sizzling beam of green light shot out from the front of the snowmobile, traveled over his shoulder and flew upwards into the sky. Timonen was an easy target, and he knew it. Another beam burst out, and another, all of them missing him by fractions. That was enough for Albrecht. He leapt out of hiding

and ran straight towards Timonen. Saar followed his lead, and with just feet to go before they ran into him, they threw themselves to either side of the big yeti.

Albrecht rolled through the snow and leapt up as the whirring snowmobile shot past. He threw himself at the vehicle, his tough fingers clutching at a metallic tow bar on the back. The churning tank tracks threw up ice-cold slush into his face, and he did all he could to hold on.

Meanwhile, Saar had tumbled to his left. When he jumped

 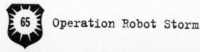

to his feet, he cast his staff out horizontally and with lightning-fast yeti reactions, swung it across the front of the snowmobile. The robots had no time to react as the staff caught their necks and knocked them flying off their seats.

The robots bounced over Albrecht, who pulled himself up to grip the handlebars. The snowmobile jittered and bobbled from left to right. By the time Albrecht got himself upright and took control, the only place it was headed was the large rock they'd been hiding behind.

"Stinking yaks!" yelled Albrecht, diving away at the very last

second before the vehicle careened into the rock at breakneck speed. The snowmobile exploded in a ball of orange flames, sending a column of smoke into the sky.

"That's done it," said Saar. "If the tower of sheep hadn't already pinpointed our position, the whole world knows it now."

Saar was crouching down on his staff, pinning the two robots to the floor by their shoulders. Timonen was pacing back and forth, slightly out of breath from his recent run. The robots shocked them both by starting to talk.

"Contact made," said the left robot in a jittery, monotone voice.

"Scanning…" said the right robot in a deeper monotone voice.

"Urgent Greebo assistance required," said the left robot.

"Strange life forms," said the right robot.

"Timonen," said Saar, "do something!"

"Repeat, urgent Greebo assistance required," said the left robot.

"Outpost infiltrated by intruders," said the right robot.

Timonen gripped the heads of the robots, one in each hand, and with a great growling effort pulled them free of their bodies. Sparks flickered from the ends of their necks, two wisps of smoke drifted upwards, and with a gentle whirr, the lights in their eyes died.

"What was all that Greebo nonsense?" said Timonen.

"We've got company," said Albrecht, appearing at their side. His fur was looking slightly charred, and his pupils were swimming in his eyes. With the snow falling ever harder, the three yetis could see a whole troop of robots mustering beside the ruined building. The blue dots of their eyes twinkled like Christmas tree lights.

"My turn to do some fancy stuff," said Timonen.

The giant yeti pounded across the snowy ground and was ecstatic to see the robots running at him. There were no lasers this time, only pickaxes and shovels, but these were useless against the power of Timonen. The robots and the yeti collided in a storm of fur and metal. Two gigantic fists lashed out and pummeled the human-sized attackers into oblivion, one after the other flying through the air as though hit by a rampaging bull.

Albrecht and Saar watched in awe as Timonen finished off the robots in a flurry of sparks and smoke.

"I admit it," said Saar, "he does have his uses."

"So these robots have opened up the old mines," said Albrecht.

"Which begs a few questions," said Saar. "Where have they come from, and who are they working for? Who would have such advanced technology?"

Despite the ruined appearance of the building from the outside, the interior had been cleaned up and strengthened by steel girders and a roof attached halfway up the wall. It was nearly weatherproof, although a wind was whistling through the extra-wide doorway and gaps in the stone walls. The yetis soon found the source of the smoke: A gleaming new engine had been set up within the ruin. It was powering cables up and down the open mineshafts below, while huffing and puffing and spewing out a thick gray exhaust into the air.

"They were digging for coal," said Saar, picking up a piece of rich black rock from the floor.

"I guess it's for power," said Albrecht.

"And it looks like they need lots of it!" added Timonen.

While his herd of sheep clustered around the engine for warmth, Timonen opened an iron door into a vast chamber quarried into the mountain. Mounds of coal rose up to its roof.

"These robots are interesting creations," said Saar. "They use a technology more advanced than we could dream of, so why do they need such an old-fashioned power source as coal?"

"Too many questions and not enough answers," said Albrecht.

He took the RoAR from his backpack and tried to find a signal in order to contact Captain Ponkerton. There wasn't even a twitch on the gray screen.

"Looks like we might as well give up on outside help," he said.

"But the robots had a signal," said Saar.

"Really?" said Albrecht, scrunching his brow.

"They alerted the other robots to our presence before Timonen pulled their heads off," he said. "It would be sensible to assume that there are probably more of them out there."

The three yetis growled as one.

"And the blizzard's getting heavier," said Timonen, his head level with one of the windows.

Snow was now forcing its way into the building through the doorway, and outside, a sloping wall of snow was growing by the second, blocking the entrance.

"It's much, much worse," said Albrecht.

Saar made a grumbling noise and walked to the doorway. It was almost pitch-black outside, but for the thick snowflakes which were falling like meteorites.

"This is no normal weather," he said. "It's freaky – just like our very own Timonen."

"Watch it, mystic!" said Timonen.

The wall of snow in the doorway was now over waist-high, and

 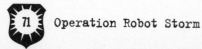

Albrecht joined Saar to watch it layer up before their eyes. The storm was unlike anything they'd experienced in the Himalayas.

"It's as though someone's targeting us with this weather," he said.

He reached out to scoop at the snow with his fingers, but he got a nasty shock. Not only was the wall now head-high, it was also impenetrable.

"It's frozen to ice," he said, and banged his fist into it.

"There's nothing else for it, then," said Timonen. "Time to eat."

"Eat? At a time like this?!" growled Albrecht.

Timonen nestled down amongst the mountain sheep to soak in some of their warmth.

"Food and rest," he said. "Once I've had those, I'll start digging. I'll get us out, you'll see."

"Fine," said Albrecht. "We'll rest for an hour, but that's all."

The yetis gobbled down their snack, Saar eating dried fruit from Albrecht's backpack while the others enjoyed dried meat. One by one, intoxicated by the warmth of the engine and the food in their bellies, they fell asleep.

Chapter 6: Underground Adventures

"You're awake now, are you?" said a man, in a coarse, gravely voice.

Albrecht could see that he was chained up in a mine. Streaks of silvery-black lined the damp walls, which dripped continuously. He remembered his military training and resorted to the rule book. The first rule of engagement with humans: Play dumb, pretend you're an animal.

"Just like the others," said the man. "Not a peep to say."

Albrecht snorted, flared his nostrils and made a sad wail of a growl. He'd moved on to the second rule of human engagement, only to be used if rule one failed: Stay calm and show a little of your sharp teeth.

"I never thought I'd see the likes of you," said the man, standing up. He took a few steps closer and swung the lamp right in front of Albrecht's eyes. "But then these are strange times…"

Albrecht blinked uncontrollably and turned his head away so

 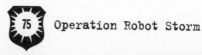

that he wasn't blinded. The man poked him on the shoulder.

"Would make a nice coat," he said. "Now that things are a bit colder on the mountain."

Albrecht gulped. It was time for the third rule of human engagement: Treat the human like an idiot.

"I'd quite like my coat to remain where it is, thanks," said Albrecht.

The old man jumped back in shock, his mouth as wide as a football. He wasn't expecting the creature to speak, let alone with a perfect English accent.

"You can talk!" he said, before hobbling away in a great hurry. "I must get help!"

Albrecht was thrown into darkness.

"Of course I can talk!" shouted the yeti in frustration.

He sat back and waited, his temper growing hotter by the second. When the old man returned, he was accompanied by a young boy and a little girl. The boy had black hair, and his scruffy clothes were completely covered in dirt and grime. Only his bright-green eyes gleamed in the darkness. He was carrying Albrecht's backpack.

"That's your help?" said Albrecht sarcastically.

"See!" said the old man to the boy. "I told you he could talk!"

The young girl rushed to Albrecht and stared at him with wide-open eyes. She was only a few years old, and she was wearing a long dress, which was equally as dirty as the boy's clothes. She stretched out her hand, touched the yeti's nose with a finger and immediately pulled it back as though it was attached to a spring.

"Cadi, that's enough," said the boy. "Come back here."

The girl ran to hide behind the old man's legs.

"My name's Gruff," said the boy.

"Albrecht," replied the yeti.

"That sounds German," said Gruff. "Are you German?"

"Do I *look* German?" said Albrecht. "It's a code name, of course."

"He's a tricky one, Gruff," said the old man. "Be careful with him!"

"Granddad!" growled the boy. He walked over to Albrecht and knelt down in front of him to speak. "Why haven't your friends said a word? I've been watching them for the past hour, but they haven't made a peep."

 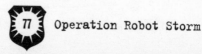

"Because there are rules for this sort of thing," said Albrecht.

"Rules?" said Gruff.

"Look," snapped Albrecht, "are you going to release us?"

Gruff shuffled back a little.

"You're something to do with those robots, aren't you?" he said inquisitively.

"No, we're nothing to do with them," said Albrecht, and he leaned forward to look closer at the boy. "But what do *you* know about them?"

"That would be telling," replied the boy.

Their eyes locked.

"Your backpack," said Gruff, "where'd you get it?"

"Mind your own business!"

"Are you from space?"

"No!"

"Australia?"

"Definitely not."

"I reckon they're monsters," said the old man.

"Monsters?!" yelled Albrecht.

"Abominable snowmen," added the old man.

"How dare you!" said Albrecht.

The boy paused for a moment. His approach wasn't working.

"Look," he said. "If we hadn't cut a hole through the ice, the fumes of that engine would have killed you."

"Is that what happened?" said Albrecht, realizing what a narrow escape they'd had.

"When the robots appeared, so did the ice," said the old man.

"So who are you?" said Albrecht. "And why haven't you gone somewhere warmer?"

"We're mountain people," said the old man. "And you won't catch us leaving our homes for a spot of bad weather!"

"I think we all realize it's more than just bad weather," said Albrecht.

"Then what is it?" said the boy.

"That's what we're trying to find out," said Albrecht. "Give me my backpack, and I'll attempt to explain. You'll have to unchain me, of course," he added hopefully.

Gruff looked suspicious.

"Look," said Albrecht. "Press that blue button on top of the backpack."

 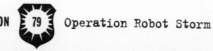

Gruff cautiously did as he said, and the RoAR popped out from under a metal cover. He held it like it was a thing of magic.

"Is it a new Game Boy?" he asked excitedly.

"Um, no," said Albrecht. "Now flick that switch across and pull out the aerial."

Gruff did as he was told, and the blank screen buzzed into life. A crackling noise came from the speaker, and then a few words shot out.

"Albrecht? Fzzzzzz… Is… Fzzzzzz … you?"

It was Captain Ponkerton! Albrecht felt a wave of relief. It had been a long shot, but there was the Captain's voice fizzing out of the speaker.

"Bang it on the floor," said Albrecht.

"What?" said Gruff.

"Bang it!"

Gruff knocked it on the ground, and a grainy picture of the Captain sprang onto the screen.

"Hello!" said Ponkerton, the signal suddenly stronger. "And who are you?"

"Don't worry!" said Albrecht. "I'm here."

"Albrecht!" said the Captain sternly. "You realize you've broken every rule going. Engagement with humans is irresponsible, not to mention forbidden!"

"When your arms and legs are chained," he replied, "and your life's at stake, you find you have very little choice in the matter."

"Ah," replied Ponkerton. "It's like that, is it? Well, see here, young man. Albrecht is a secret agent of the British Army. He's on your side, so please let him go about his business."

"Why should I believe you?" said Gruff.

"Look at the handle of the device you're holding," said Ponkerton.

Gruff read the few small words stamped onto the handle: PROPERTY OF THE BRITISH ARMED FORCES.

"Right," said Gruff.

"Now would you pass me over to Albrecht, please."

Gruff held the RoAR in front of the yeti so he could see the screen.

"You ran into trouble, then?" said Ponkerton.

"We met some robots…"

"Ahhh," said Ponkerton.

"You say that like you know something," said Albrecht.

"You remember that last call, when I got cut off?" said Ponkerton.

Albrecht peered at Gruff and the old man, who were watching him intently.

"Yes," he said to the screen.

"It wasn't only our signal that was cut off," said the Captain. "All the television signals in the world were cut off."

"How?"

"You might want to prepare yourself," said Ponkerton.

"I'm prepared!"

"Right, then. The situation is much, much worse than we could ever have imagined."

"That bad?" said Albrecht.

"Worse than bad. When the signals were cut, another signal took their place and was sent to every radio and TV across the globe. Because you're on a fixed loop, you wouldn't have received this message…"

The picture on the RoAR switched to a video of a man

whose face was nearly fully covered by a round hood. Only his eyes and the bridge of his nose could be seen, circled by blue material. Behind him were two robots, just like those the yetis had fought earlier, carrying laser guns.

Somewhere beneath the hood, the man's mouth must have been moving because words started to come through the speaker.

"My name is Balaclava," he said. "Remember it. Say it loud because you'll be hearing it a lot."

"Who is he?" said Gruff.

Albrecht shuddered and raised his hand for the boy to stop talking. He carried on listening.

"The world is about to change," continued Balaclava. "Through my own hard work and brilliance, I have created this planet's first weather machine. It is a work of genius! And to demonstrate its effectiveness, I have set about freezing the small country of Wales. Rest assured this is merely a fraction of the new power I have at my disposal, so unless you want more countries to undergo a similar fate, consider my demands carefully.

"Governments of the world, you face a choice. To buy your continued safety, I am willing to accept the small fee of

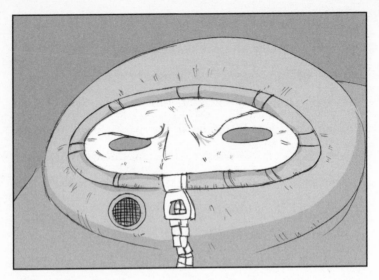

ONE TRILLION DOLLARS. This will be handed over to me in cash at a location of my choosing. However, if you decide to ignore my demand then I will bring a new Ice Age to the entire planet. You have until midnight on Friday to hand over the money.

"Good night, world! Sleep tight."

The RoAR's screen flicked back to Captain Ponkerton.

Albrecht was speechless.

"Albrecht," said Ponkerton. "You can see how grave this matter is. There is no way the British government can afford

 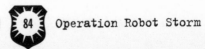

to pay their share of the ransom and neither can the rest of the world. So, you see, your rescue mission truly has become a quest to save the planet. Today *is* Friday. You've got until midnight to find Balaclava and put that weather machine out of action. You three yetis are our only hope."

"Abominable snowmen!" declared the old man. "I told you!"

"We don't like to use that term anymore," said Ponkerton. "It's rather outdated and frankly, quite rude."

"But what can we do about this?" said Albrecht. "We don't know anything about Balaclava. We don't even know *where* he is!"

"Actually," said Ponkerton, "we've got good leads on both of those."

"Go on…"

"We traced his signal to the heart of the storm over Snowdonia. We think it may have even come from Mount Snowdon itself. But as you know, we can't see through the cloud cover to get a better look."

"So if we're going stop him, we need to head into the storm?" asked Albrecht.

 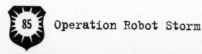

"There's no doubt about it. And as for who he is... Remember the Arctic Iceberg Incident?"

Albrecht blushed beneath his fur. The Mythical 9th Division was often used as an advance scouting party, secretly plotting and mapping terrain before the real army could arrive. During that mission, while charting a cluster of icebergs, a particularly frisky lady polar bear had paid him a little more attention than was healthy.

"I remember all too well," he said.

"We now think that it might have been Balaclava who was shearing off icebergs and driving them into the shipping fleets."

"But that was Dr. Icepick," said Albrecht.

"Correct," said Ponkerton, "but during the cleanup we found numerous technical plans for robots at his secret hide-out. The similarities between them and the robots who stood behind him in the broadcast are striking. Balaclava and Dr. Icepick could well be the same man."

"This gets worse by the second," said Albrecht.

The boy removed a set of keys from his waist and unchained the yeti. He'd heard enough to know this was big.

"Thank you, young man," said Ponkerton. "Now, Albrecht, get the others and find this evil mastermind. I fear we have very little time."

"Yes, sir," said Albrecht. "We'll do our best."

As the RoAR went blank, Albrecht stretched out and stood up, standing tall over the humans.

"Thanks," said the yeti. "Where are the other two?"

"This way," said Gruff, "but I'd best show you something first."

Albrecht was taken through a tunnel into a cavernous area with wooden scaffolding all around. Lamps and torches hung from the walls, casting an orange glow onto the floor. Piles of canned food and bottled water lay around, and a few of the lost sheep that Timonen had rescued were resting on the floor.

"Look," said Gruff, pointing to a wall while his sister, Cadi, clung to his leg in terror.

One of Balaclava's robots was standing upright, facing into the room. There were no lights in its eyes.

"It's a big one," said Gruff. "Bigger than the others, at any rate. These are the only ones we've seen with lasers."

Albrecht walked closer and tapped the robot's head. Its body was just the same as those of the first two robots they'd encountered. It had slightly different facial features and thicker arms and legs than the other type.

"We think this one was a leader," said Gruff. "We'd been watching the robots all day yesterday, when it suddenly keeled over. Granddad's had a look at it, and he reckons it short-circuited."

Albrecht examined the robot, pulling at flaps of metal, pressing in parts that looked like buttons.

"Its head comes apart," said the old man. "Just a screw underneath that metal band…"

The old man took a penknife from his pocket, and with a little fiddling, the robot's head flipped in half to reveal a block of wires and circuit boards placed securely at its center.

"It does come out, if you pull it," he said.

The yeti dived right in and withdrew the unit of circuit boards completely. He noticed an open socket on its side and a line of writing inscribed next to it.

"General Robotic Electronically Enhanced Battle Outfit, 2000 model," said Albrecht, reading the writing. "G-R-E-E-B-O. So that's it! It's a Greebo!"

Albrecht switched on his RoAR and uncoiled a cable from the base of its handle. The end of the cable fitted the socket perfectly, and the yeti plugged the two together. The old man was clearly impressed.

"Universal adapter," said Albrecht, smiling. "This thing works anywhere."

On the RoAR's screen, line after line of digits scrolled down the display. Albrecht was good with technology, but it read like gibberish. Eventually the flow of numbers slowed to a stop, and Albrecht disconnected the boards.

"I'll send this information to the Captain," he said, pressing a button, "and see if his specialists come up with anything."

"Handy, that thing," said the old man.

"When it works," replied Albrecht.

Suddenly there was a scuffle above them, and a chunk of icy snow fell to the ground from a hole in the ceiling. A rope dropped down, and a pair of heavily booted feet appeared.

THE MYTHICAL **9th** DIVISION

ITEM: GREEBO 1000
SERIAL No: 5671-63/YETI
STATUS: *TOP-SECRET*

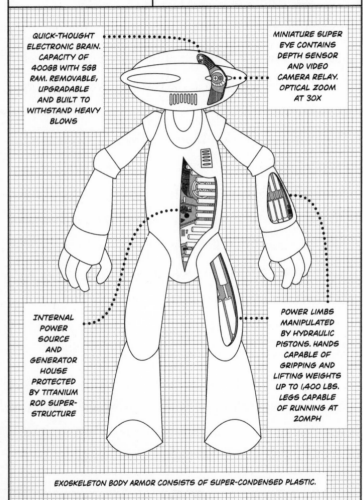

QUICK-THOUGHT ELECTRONIC BRAIN. CAPACITY OF 400GB WITH 5GB RAM. REMOVABLE, UPGRADABLE AND BUILT TO WITHSTAND HEAVY BLOWS

MINIATURE SUPER EYE CONTAINS DEPTH SENSOR AND VIDEO CAMERA RELAY. OPTICAL ZOOM AT 30X

INTERNAL POWER SOURCE AND GENERATOR HOUSE PROTECTED BY TITANIUM ROD SUPER-STRUCTURE

POWER LIMBS MANIPULATED BY HYDRAULIC PISTONS. HANDS CAPABLE OF GRIPPING AND LIFTING WEIGHTS UP TO 1,400 LBS. LEGS CAPABLE OF RUNNING AT 20MPH

EXOSKELETON BODY ARMOR CONSISTS OF SUPER-CONDENSED PLASTIC.

"Hold it right there, buster," said a woman, who was quickly sliding down the rope. She was followed by a number of other humans, all wrapped in multiple layers of clothes and sheets for warmth.

"Mum!" said Gruff, happy to see her return.

Cadi ran from her brother and gripped her mother's hand.

"Gruff! Cadi! What did I tell you two about running off like that?" she said.

"Aw, but Mum, it's OK. They work for the British Army, and they're here to *save* us. They're yetis!"

The woman unwrapped the material from her face to get a better look.

"Well, I've seen some strange things of late," she replied, "but yetis?!"

"We originally came to rescue some British soldiers," said Albrecht. "But now it seems we're here to save the world."

"Then it's nice to meet you," said Gruff's mum. "I'm Ang."

"Albrecht," said Albrecht. "And it's not the first time this sort of thing has happened—"

"There's a criminal mastermind on Snowdon," Gruff

interrupted. "His name's Balaclava, and he's the one who made the glaciers."

"A criminal mastermind?" said Ang.

"It's true," said the old man. "We saw it all on that yeti's little TV!"

"Well, I'd love to help," said Ang, "but we don't have much here apart from mining tools."

"I appreciate the offer," said Albrecht, "but we really just need to get through the storm."

"The storm?" said Ang. "You'll be lucky. Only the robots can get through that. I've watched them. They can enter on their snowmobiles – they seem to have a storm-resistant force field around them – but there's no other way. It's like a wall of wind, ice and snow, stretching from the ground to the sky. It'll freeze you on entry."

Albrecht was worried about this, but he had the expectations of the whole world on his shoulders. He didn't want to give the wrong impression.

"We're yetis," he said confidently. "We're built for these things."

* * *

Timonen barely fitted into the mine shaft. He'd been dragged unconscious through the tunnels until the humans could pull him no further, and when he'd woken up, he'd found his shoulders were as wide as the walls were narrow.

With a lone sheep wandering beside him, Saar walked up to his friend and unlocked the chains around his arms and legs.

"Now, don't do anything rash," said Saar.

Timonen had a face like thunder.

"Just you watch," he said. "I'm going to squash these little people's heads between my fingertips!"

Albrecht appeared in the tunnel, followed by Gruff and the other humans. More of the sheep that Timonen had rescued were behind them.

"Timonen!" said Albrecht. "Relax!"

"Don't tell me to relax," he replied, his huge hands clutching at the walls of the tunnel and digging into the earth. "I'll show them—"

"Timonen, stop," said Saar calmly.

Clouds of steam were blasting out of Timonen's nose. His

temper was building. Suddenly Cadi ran out from behind Gruff and leapt into the dense fur of Timonen's leg. Her arms only reached halfway around his calf, but she gripped hold of his long hair while standing on his foot.

"Fluffy," she said, giggling.

Timonen's grip on the walls weakened, and his bad temper deflated in an instant.

"Oh, all right!" he said gruffly, trying not to look pleased. "Get me out of here, now!"

"Which way's out?" Saar asked Ang.

"I'll show you to the glacier," said Gruff, before his mother could say anything.

"Oh, no, you won't!" said Ang. "They can go by themselves."

"Aw, Mum!" he pleaded, looking embarrassed.

"No," she said firmly. "It's not safe. They can manage without your help."

"Look," said Albrecht, wading into the row. "Take this…"

He passed the boy a small metal device, which had a screen and a few buttons on its front.

"It's a GRoWL," said Albrecht. "Even if you're not with

us, you can be a part of the mission."

"It looks like a mobile phone!" said Gruff. "Mum won't let me have one of those."

Ang rolled her eyes.

"Ah ... but you'll only get me on it," said Albrecht. "It's to keep me informed of what's happening in the mines."

"Sure, sure," said Gruff, pressing one of the buttons on its front. Albrecht's backpack buzzed loudly.

"See?" said Albrecht.

"Excellent!" said the boy.

"So you're staying here," said Ang finally.

Gruff nodded reluctantly.

"This way," said Ang to the yetis. "I'll show you the way out."

* * *

The Mythical 9th Division emerged into a bright, moonlit world, high up on the hillside above the mine. Albrecht had filled them in on the new turn of events, and they understood the task at hand. Across the rivers of ice they could see the swirling, pure black cloud towering over the glacier and blotting out the stars.

"There's the storm front," said Saar. "Only one way to go now!"

"Yes, but how on earth are we going to get through it?" said Albrecht.

"Don't worry – I have a plan," said Saar mysteriously.

And with that, they paced down the side of the hill until they reached the glacier again. The ice was covered in a thick layer of snow, but not nearly enough to bother a huge yeti like Timonen. He set off, spooning piles of snow to his side as he went.

"Come on, Albrecht," said Saar. "We should make the most of our very own furry snowplow."

THE MYTHICAL 9th DIVISION

Chapter 7: Into the Storm

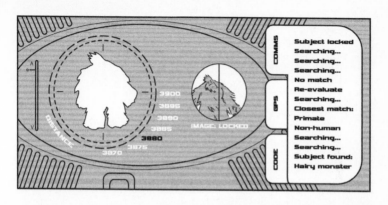

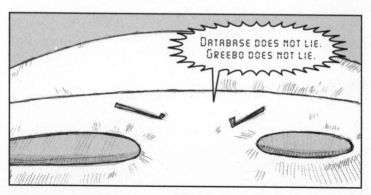

THEN YOUR SOFTWARE CLEARLY NEEDS AN UPGRADE. GET BETTER IMAGES OF THE SUSPECTS.

GREEBO?

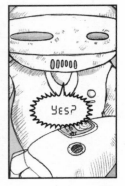

YES?

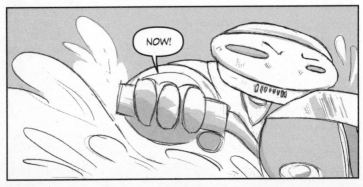

NOW!

MEANWHILE...

The sun was rising, but no light could be seen through the massive anvil-shaped storm cloud that filled the horizon. Just a hundred yards away, from the surface of the glacier to the top of the sky, the black storm cloud swirled violently, consuming everything around it. The air temperature dropped ever lower as the storm cloud moved towards the Mythical 9th.

"In yeti terms, I'd say that was lunker," said Timonen, standing firm against the powerful wind.

Saar slammed the base of his staff into the snow and sat down. He draped his scarf across his legs and closed his eyes.

"What's he doing that for?" said Timonen.

Albrecht took the binoculars from his backpack and zoomed in on the cloud.

"I imagine he's meditating on it," he said. "You know him."

"Albrecht," mumbled Saar, from the ground. "We need to enter the storm front. The only way we can survive is by being at one with the elements."

He clutched his staff, and the wood took on a faint glow as an ancient magical power ran through it.

"We must use the Way of the Yeti."

"Oh, no," said Timonen. "He's really gone and lost it now."

"The key is to control your body," said Saar. "Lower your inner temperature using your mind. Slow your breathing to save energy. Feel the storm within you."

"I don't believe I'm hearing this," said Timonen. "Last time he was telling me I could float if I became one with the air, now he's telling me to be one with this storm cloud!"

"Sit down," said Saar, sweeping his staff into Timonen's ankles and sending him crashing to the floor.

"You could have asked," Timonen fumed, a cloud of steam rising into the air from his nostrils.

"Oh, stop fighting!" snapped Albrecht.

A slight smile appeared on Saar's otherwise still face.

"Join me," he said, "and close your eyes."

Timonen growled at Albrecht, who was giving him one of his do-as-I-say looks. He knew he had no choice.

"All right," grumbled Timonen.

Albrecht sat down next to Saar and shut his eyes.

"Breathe deeply," said Saar calmly. "Feel the cold outside you and welcome it in."

Their breathing grew slower, and their fur sank as though the wind had lost its grip.

"The Way of the Yeti is in you," said Saar mystically. "Clutch the Staff of Ages and feel its power."

Saar held the staff horizontally in front of him, and the other yetis took hold. The world grew dark around them as they fell into a trance. Long, wintry tendrils reached out from the storm cloud as it reached the spot where the yetis were sitting. Suddenly a bright flash of blue lightning forked through the sky and hit Saar's staff. The ground shook, and a massive booming explosion rumbled through the air.

The storm had hit them.

The Greebo watched from the glacier as the yetis were enveloped in the storm. His three-fingered hand clutched the handlebars of his snowmobile, and with the flick of a switch, he was in contact with Balaclava once more.

"Three intruders inside storm barrier," said the robot.

"What!" yelled Balaclava. "How can that be!?"

"Human boy also crossing glacier. Following intruders."

"These intruders, did you get a good look at them?"

"Processing image," said the Greebo. "Sending now."

There was a moment of quiet.

"Awaiting orders," said the robot.

"Yes, yes. Wait," said Balaclava.

The Greebo waited.

"May the ice freeze my heart!" said Balaclava. "If I didn't know better, I'd say they were yetis."

"Yeti does not compute. No yeti specification on file."

"That's because they're mythical beasts," said Balaclava. "They *do not* exist. Get me that boy. I want to question him."

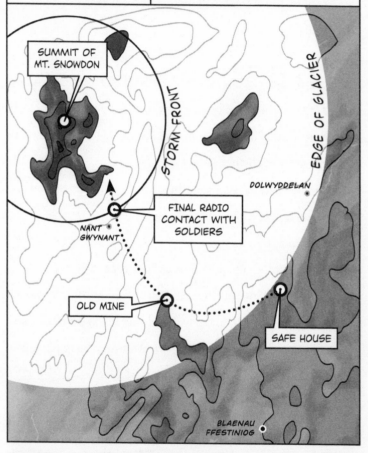

"Order understood," said the Greebo, revving up the snow-mobile's engine.

"And I want to know if those creatures make it through the barrier alive!"

Albrecht opened his eyes. He could feel nothing. He hadn't moved, but he could tell he was now inside the menacing cloud. An ice storm raged all around, and sharp, dagger-like crystals plummeted from the blackened sky.

"Stand up," said Saar, struggling to be heard over the howling wind. "You're having an out-of-body experience. It should feel like you're in a dream."

Albrecht stood up and felt lighter than air. Everything seemed to work fine, but he felt weird. Beside him, Timonen was in a total daze. The snow was building up on his back like a layer of frosty icing, and he couldn't feel a thing. Saar, of course, felt fine.

"I suppose we should make a move," said Albrecht, taking the RoAR from his backpack to check their direction.

Suddenly a bolt of lightning seared down through the clouds

and struck Timonen. His fur sizzled, his eyes lit up, and his arms and legs shot outwards.

"Ummm," he said, as his fur began to lie flat, and the last twinkles of electricity flickered from his eyes. "Should that have hurt?"

"Unfortunately," said Saar, "you'll feel the effects later, once you rejoin your body."

"Rejoin my body?" said Timonen quietly. "I don't understand."

"I didn't think you would," said Saar.

Albrecht noticed that Timonen's hair had changed color, from bronze to white. He decided not to mention it.

"He's far more tolerable when he's calm like this," said Saar, walking away steadily.

"He won't be happy when he snaps out of it though," said Albrecht. "Actually, when *will* we snap out of it?"

Saar strode on across the glacier, the horrendous weather playing out around him.

"It'll be a gradual thing," he said. "But you'll know when you're free of it."

Albrecht checked the RoAR once more. The light of the screen beamed out in the gloom, displaying the map of the terrain. They were on course. He returned the device to his backpack and then unlatched a lamp which he strapped around his head.

Like a lighthouse in the dark, Albrecht wandered into the dense, misty elements, keeping track of the other yetis by the beam of light protruding from his head.

"Are we cold?" asked Albrecht.

"Freezing, I should imagine," said Saar.

"And it won't hurt us?"

"Of course it'll hurt," said Saar. "Although we won't feel anything like as bad as Timonen will, once we're through."

"Wonderful," said Timonen.

Through the gloom, Albrecht spotted something, picked up by the light from his head lamp. He held out his hand in a stop sign, and the yetis dropped to the ground in an instant.

"Could be Greebos," he said.

Albrecht reduced the beam of his lamp to a dull glow and crawled forward. He stopped about fifty yards ahead of

the others and peered into the darkness. There were strange shapes bulging out of the glacier. He waited, looking for movement, but when none came he continued to crawl forward. After a few more yards, Albrecht realized what he'd found.

With a flick of his wrist, his head lamp lit up again, and Albrecht stood up, beaming the light over his discovery. He motioned for the other yetis to join him.

In front of them were the lost soldiers of the British Army. Frozen into blocks of ice, the troops looked as though they were suspended in time. Some were running, some were falling, others were screaming and shouting, but they were all trapped in the thick, glass-like ice.

"One mystery solved," said Saar grimly.

"Are they dead?" asked Timonen.

Saar placed the Staff of Ages against their icy cage. The end of the staff glowed dimly.

"They're alive," he said, "but for how long, I don't know."

Chapter 8: The Eye of the Storm

THE YETIS MAKE FOR THE SUMMIT OF MT. SNOWDON

Saar gave a shivery groan, and his fingers started to tremble.

"Hold on," he said, his voice wobbling.

Albrecht realized the Way of the Yeti was leaving them. His body felt as though it had been cast into a deep freeze, and then fast as lightning, the icy chill shot upwards through his bones and vanished. He felt totally exhausted.

Timonen was watching his friends readjust to normality, wondering what all the fuss was about, when suddenly his eyes opened wide. His body shook uncontrollably, and the loudest roar Albrecht had ever heard burst from his lips. It echoed around the mountain, bouncing off rocks and icy lakes. His fur bristled and then settled down as he regained a kind of composure.

"Feeling better?" said Saar.

Timonen looked as though his head was spinning. The aftereffects of being struck by lightning had finally hit him.

"Nooooo," he moaned, shivering. He slumped to the ground.

Albrecht removed his backpack and lifted a panel on its base. He pulled out a small bottle which, with a turn of its cap, started to froth.

"Drink this!" he said.

"What is it?" said Timonen.

"Medicated yaks' milk. It's my grandmother's special recipe for mountain injuries."

"What?" said Timonen.

He took the bottle and sniffed the contents.

"It smells of dead things!"

"Drink it!" said Albrecht. "You'll feel better."

Timonen took the delicate bottle between two huge fingers and downed the frothy contents in one sip. His eyes glowed yellow for a moment, and his cheek fur turned pink where his skin was flushing red below.

"Better?" asked Saar, reveling in Timonen's misfortune.

The big yeti burped, hiccuped and was violently sick on Saar's feet.

"Much better," he replied.

Timonen soon found his legs again.

"So where's Balaclava?" he grumbled, standing up. "It's time for him to taste some yeti fist!"

Albrecht shrugged his shoulders. "Who knows?" he replied. "But standing around here won't help find him."

The yetis walked to where the mountain poked out of the glacier and followed a narrow path that wound upwards along a thin ridge of rock. They marched on, gaining height all the while, but noticed nothing unusual until the sound of a grumbling motor took their attention down on the ice sheet.

Albrecht pulled out his binoculars and zoomed in on a snowmobile leaving the storm and crossing the icy ground towards the mountain. A faint white glow surrounded the vehicle like a protective shield – the force field Ang had told them about. "It's a Greebo!" said Albrecht. Then, as he looked closer, he spotted a body on the back of the craft. "And it looks like he's got someone with him!"

"Who?" said Saar.

A boy sat on the back of the snowmobile, tied to the handle-bars and wrapped from head to toe in layers of clothes. He had thick gloves covering his hands and sturdy leather boots. The rest of him was a bundle of ill-fitting shirts and trousers, topped off with a sprawl of tablecloth for good measure.

"It's a small human," said Albrecht. "Oh, no, you don't think—"

"Gruff?" said Saar. "Is he all right?"

"I don't know. Let's follow it, see where it goes," said Albrecht. "Come on!"

The snowmobile clung close to the base of the mountain,

skipping over the icy glacial peaks like a speedboat over waves. Eventually it sped out of sight, and Albrecht slid down the rocky slope until he could see it again. The snowmobile was now surrounded by a number of larger Greebos.

"More robots," said Albrecht, looking through his binoculars. "The same as that one in the mine."

Timonen snatched the binoculars to get a better look himself. His eyes were so far apart that he could only see through one eyepiece.

"Well, if there are more of them, they'll be more fun to fight," he said. "They might even put up a struggle this time!"

"What are they doing with the boy?" said Saar.

The Greebos pulled Gruff from the back of the vehicle, then carried him into the mountain through an entrance that was out of the yetis' line of sight. A Greebo revved up the snowmobile's engine and followed them in.

"They've gone in," said Timonen. "How am I supposed to pummel them now?"

Albrecht leapt another few feet down the slope to the next flat level.

 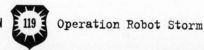

"I'm going down," he said. "Wait here while I check it out."

Albrecht scrambled down the slope with one hand scraping along the ground to steady himself. He jumped the final stretch and landed primed and ready on the snow-covered floor. His eyes darted once from left to right, then he looked straight ahead at the gigantic set of doors made of pure blue ice. They were set into the charcoal-gray rock of the mountain, and numerous tracks and messy footprints were dotted in the snow in front of them.

Albrecht lifted his arm and signaled for his friends to join him. Timonen wasted no time. He cleared the distance in one huge leap and crashed down beside his friend. Saar took slightly longer, steadying himself with his staff as he slid to the glacier.

With the Mythical 9th Division ready for action, Albrecht tightened his backpack.

"OK, Timonen," he said, "break down that door!"

Timonen rubbed his hands and scuffed his feet along the ground to build up steam. He charged shoulder-first at the doors and with an almighty thud, smashed into them.

Usually Timonen broke things without trying, but this time he collapsed onto the snowy floor with ripples of pain coursing through his body. The doors stayed exactly where they were.

"They're not budging," he said, clutching his arm.

"Greebo 2000, bring him here!" ordered Balaclava.

The criminal mastermind sat in a chair made of ice, with his back to the room. He stared at a wall of TV displays, watching news from around the world flash and flicker on the screens. Occasional glimpses of the newly formed Welsh glaciers popped up, but it wasn't enough for him. A timer above the screens was counting down to midnight, ready for when Balaclava became rich beyond his wildest dreams, or the world suffered an icy demise.

Gruff tripped over his own feet as he was shoved forward.

"Who are you?" said Gruff nervously, wishing he'd never run away from the mines.

Balaclava spun around in his seat. He was clothed from head to toe in a puffy, all-in-one blue snowsuit, and a zipper ran all the way from his waist up to his nose. Only his eyes and eyebrows were visible through the circular space left empty by his all-enveloping...

"Balaclava!" said Gruff.

"So, my name precedes me!" he replied, standing up. Balaclava may have been a criminal mastermind, but he was very short: no taller than the boy.

Balaclava prowled around the control room, his eyes focused on Gruff. The Greebo stepped forward and passed a metal box to the evil genius.

"Prisoner's possessions," said the Greebo.

It was the GRoWL. Balaclava took it and held it behind his back as he continued to circle the boy.

"These furry creatures you were in pursuit of," he said, in a sugary voice. "Tell me about them."

Gruff flinched. He knew he wasn't supposed to say a word.

"I don't know what you're talking about," he said.

Balaclava laughed.

"Of course you do," he said. "I can tell you're lying from the way your eye is twitching."

"I'm not lying," said the boy, trying to be brave, but inwardly feeling rather terrified.

Balaclava nodded to the Greebo, and the robot walked out of the room.

"I presume you're one of those humans from the mine," said Balaclava, changing tack.

"No, I'm not!" snapped Gruff.

"Good," said Balaclava. "Then it won't matter to you if I decide to … rid myself of that little problem."

"But they're not doing any harm!" said Gruff foolishly.

"They're not?" said Balaclava slowly.

He finally took a look at the GRoWL. Intrigued, he inspected it closely, taking in every detail. Then he froze. His eyes had landed on something very important.

"Where did you get this from?" he asked.

Gruff shrugged. "I found it on the mountain," he said.

"Ah, did you?" said Balaclava. "Then you won't mind if I have a little play with it? I wonder what happens if I press this—"

"No!" said Gruff, but it was too late.

The GRoWL beeped and vibrated, then a voice came through the speaker, loud and clear.

"Gruff!" said Albrecht.

Gruff seized up. Balaclava smiled.

"Is everything all right?" said Albrecht. "We're—"

"Everything's quite all right," Balaclava interrupted icily. "Especially now that I, the world's coldest man, have your little friend as a hostage. I do hope you're going to try and rescue him. Although you might find you're in for a frosty reception."

"What!? Is that Bal—?"

Balaclava pressed the button again, and Albrecht was cut off.

"Property of the British Army, it says here," said Balaclava. "So whoever you are, you're my enemy. And those yetis..."

"I don't know what you're talking about," said Gruff, unconvincingly.

"You are a particularly terrible liar!" screamed Balaclava, who was getting very angry.

Gruff clenched his fists and squeezed them really hard. He knew he should have listened to his mum, instead of following the yetis across the glacier.

Balaclava walked closer and stood face to face with him. "Prepare to feel my wrath!" He waved his hand towards the door, where the Greebo was just returning to the room, pulling a cart that carried a glistening cube of ice.

"Take a look at how you will pay for your interference, insufferable human boy!"

The sight that greeted Gruff froze his heart. Standing inside the giant ice cube, trapped as though in a piece of modern art, was a long-haired sheep.

"I had to give my Thermogun something to do," said Balaclava.

"Is it d-d-dead?" stammered Gruff.

"Oh, no," said Balaclava. "Just frozen solid. It can stay like

 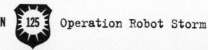

that for about a month, in a kind of sleepy state. Any longer and its brain will turn to mush. I wonder how your poor mother will feel when she sees you in the same state?"

Gruff was petrified.

"I– I–"

"Take him away," ordered Balaclava. "And send out patrols to find those miners and those blasted yetis. Then get this room ready for transmission. The time for games is over."

The Greebo grabbed the boy by his wrists, then marched him from the room. Balaclava walked up to the wall of displays and pressed a button on the control panel in front. The screens went blank for a second before the image of his face appeared on every one.

"World!" exclaimed Balaclava, for he was now being broadcast on every channel on every television the world over. "I'm beginning to think you're not taking me seriously. I gave you until midnight to come to a decision. I played fair. But now, I find you've been trying to overthrow me. So now I'm going to play dirty too."

Balaclava stretched up, grabbed hold of a metal handle above his head and pulled it down. All the screens turned black, and the blue neon lighting in the room fizzed and dimmed. A deep, rumbling growl filled the air.

All at once the floor began to vibrate and move upwards. Balaclava's hands danced over the control panel, pressing button after button, turning dials from left to right and flicking switches. As the floor shuddered to a halt, Balaclava pressed a large red button surrounded by black-and-yellow warning stripes. The criminal mastermind stepped backwards, and the screens flickered back to life.

"In a few minutes," he said, "you, the world, will taste the power of the Elemental. Then you'll wish that you hadn't messed with me!" Then, almost as an afterthought, he added, "I think I'll start with London."

Albrecht returned the RoAR to his backpack.

"Balaclava's captured Gruff," he informed the others. "We have to rescue him. Who knows what that lunatic will do next?"

"I think that could be it," said Saar, stepping back. "Look up!"

Above them, the white cloud cover had thinned to nothing,

and the bright-blue sky had appeared in all its glory. All around them, the mountain was grumbling and shaking, as rocks of assorted sizes tumbled from their resting places.

"It's like we're in an earthquake," yelled Saar, as a metal structure blossomed from the mountainside, appearing like a snowdrop from the wintry ground. Its petals opened towards the sky, spreading wider by the second, until it stood fully formed.

"It's a massive satellite dish," said Albrecht.

Then the yetis' jaws dropped even lower. On the far side of the mountain, a magnificent silver-blue building had forced its way up through the rock. Its walls were angled like an upturned bucket, and massive fins of ice stretched down into the bedrock to support the structure.

The satellite dish started to move, rotating slowly as though finding its most comfortable position. As soon as it stopped, the rod at its center fizzed and sparked with flashes of electricity. The dish glowed bright-white, and a huge ray of blue light blasted into the stratosphere, momentarily connecting the earth and the sky. The mountain shook violently, and the yetis fell to the ground.

"That's not a good sign," said Albrecht.

Chapter 9: The Elemental Strikes

LONDON: TRAFALGAR SQUARE, JULY 23, 12:45 PM

MEANWHILE, BACK IN WALES...

PHUT

"**T**ime to put that dish out of action," said Albrecht. "Who knows what Balaclava's just done…"

"We have to get inside," said Saar.

Timonen rubbed his shoulder. He was determined not to be beaten.

"Those doors are mine," he growled.

The big yeti charged at the two huge doors once more, his shoulder forced out, ready to take the pain of impact. As he hit, his body crumpled, but the doors remained resolutely shut.

"Ouch," he moaned.

"I think we need a better idea," said Albrecht.

He checked his RoAR for inspiration, but it revealed nothing. The signal to Captain Ponkerton was fizzing with static.

They had been staring at the entrance for a short while when suddenly, Saar heard something.

"What's that?" he said.

In the distance, they could hear a strange *pup-pup* noise; the sound of an engine working extra hard. The noise grew louder and louder.

"Sounds like a train," said Albrecht. "But up here?" He shot a look towards Saar and then ran off.

"Come on!" he shouted, urging the others to follow him.

Albrecht scrambled back up the rocky mountainside and returned to the path they'd been following. He could see puffs of smoke rising into the air, forming a trail across the mountainside. They seemed to be heading higher, closing in on the secret base.

The three yetis ran as fast as they could, bounding over rocks and snowy outcrops and climbing upwards at an extraordinary rate. Forever watchful of the huge secret base that now sat prominently high up on the mountain, the yetis soon reached an open area, and Albrecht caught sight of what they'd been chasing.

"It *is* a train!" he exclaimed. "A really old-looking train."

"It's tiny," said Timonen. "Is everything small in Wales?"

Saar spotted the shiny material in the three short carriages behind the train.

"It's pulling minerals," he said.

"And there are just two Greebos manning it," said Albrecht.

He scanned the course of the track, following it along a ridge to a cliff face directly below Balaclava's base. A narrow tunnel had been cut into the rock, and the tracks disappeared inside.

"They're taking the raw goods into the mountain," said Albrecht. "That's our way in."

"I'm on it," said Timonen.

Before Albrecht could do anything, the big yeti sped off across the slope and caught up with the rear car. He jumped on and pulled himself along the top, his course covered by the steam puffing out of the engine's funnel. Once he'd reached it, he pushed one arm through either side of the cabin, grabbed a Greebo in each hand and clashed their heads together. Sparks flew out of their eyes, and he discarded them over his shoulders.

It was only then that Timonen realized he wouldn't fit through the doorway into the cabin; nor did he know how to drive a train.

"Flaming yaks," he said quietly. "Saar's gonna get me for this..."

 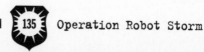

He dropped down and ran to the train's front to try and halt its movement by pushing against it. Even though it moved so slowly, the little engine was strong, and Timonen's feet were pushed backwards, bumping on each railway tie as they slipped along.

"Grrrr!" he shouted. "Albrecht! Hurry up!"

The others soon reached him and took command of the engine's controls without much hassle.

"Maybe try thinking next time," shouted Saar, pulling a handle to release more steam.

Timonen stepped aside and let the engine pass. He saluted them.

"Just get in one of the cars," said Albrecht. "And get covered."

For once, the big yeti did as he was told.

"So how are we going to sneak in unnoticed?" asked Saar, shoveling a pile of coal into the boiler's fire, making it roar louder. The track still had a few hundred yards to go before it reached the tunnel.

"We're going to pretend to be Greebos," he replied. "You

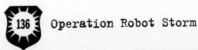

know how to do the robot dance, right?"

Saar couldn't tell if he was joking or not and looked at his friend with the blankest expression he could muster.

"Excuse me?"

"Two Greebos fallen," said a Greebo 2000.

Balaclava turned to look at the robot.

"Where? Outside the barrier or nearby?" he asked angrily. "How?"

"No shutdown signal received," came the reply.

"I knew I should have rid myself of the 1000 series," said Balaclava. "Useless, the bunch of them."

"Radar ineffective," added the Greebo. "Elemental too hot. Monitors scrambled."

"I could have told you that," grumbled Balaclava.

The evil mastermind paced around his room, watching the TV screens. They were showing views of the mountain taken by security cameras dotted all around. He glanced at the massive satellite dish, the mountain slopes, the mineral mines and even the railway. There wasn't an intruder to be seen.

"Send out a search party to recover the fallen Greebos. I want to know what happened to them. And set the base to security level three. Those yetis must be out there, and we can't take any chances."

The Greebo 2000's visor flashed red, the sign that its words would be relayed to every Greebo through the speakers on their heads.

"Security raise: level three. Security raise: level three."

Balaclava swung around on his chair. He sat quietly, thinking about his next move, when a light flashed above his displays. He leaned forward leisurely and pressed a button. The displays crackled, and as the picture stabilized, they revealed the British Prime Minister, Arthur Barnstormer.

"Good day," said Balaclava.

"It is not a good day, as you know very well," replied Barnstormer. "We order you to stop this futile freezing of our country immediately."

"Or what?" said Balaclava.

"Or you will be responsible for the deaths of millions of people!" The Prime Minister was outraged.

"That's your problem, not mine. If you'd just given me the cash," said Balaclava, "things would not be as they are now."

"But what you asked was impossible!" said Barnstormer.

"Not at all," said Balaclava. "I find people can make the impossible happen very easily now that I'm in control of a weather machine!"

"But London – indeed our whole country – is now suffering immense damage…"

"Yes, it is. But since you were the ones who double-crossed me, I don't think you have any right to complain. Now, excuse me, I have a world to glaciate. Please let your American friends know they're next for the big freeze. Goodbye."

Balaclava turned off the displays and allowed himself a maniacal laugh. He didn't do it very often, just on special occasions, but he immediately felt much better about life.

"You didn't really think robot dancing was my plan?" said Albrecht, who was squeezed into the driver's cabin alongside Saar.

"I never know with you," said Saar. "But I'm still not convinced that hiding is a better alternative."

 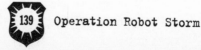

The entrance to the cave was upon them. It was only marginally wider than the train, and nobody would spot the yetis until they'd gone through.

"Once we're in, we're in," said Albrecht, smiling through gritted teeth.

The train powered on, and Albrecht watched the walls close in on them as they passed inside. Eventually the tunnel expanded into a huge cavern lit by flickering fluorescent bulbs.

"I'm not going to use the brakes," he said. "We let the train run away, and we jump out to meet whatever's waiting for us. OK?"

Saar poked his head up to look forward through the tiny round windows.

"OK," he said. "Just be prepared to run."

"That bad?" said Albrecht.

He didn't need to look through a window, he could now see through the sides of the cabin. The train was driving through a mine filled with piles of metal and rock. Greebos were working all around, pickaxes swinging down every few seconds, dinging and clanging against the bare rock.

"Right, then," said Albrecht. "After you."

 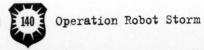

The two yetis nodded at each other, and Saar leapt from his side of the engine, shortly followed by Albrecht. Timonen had been waiting anxiously for them, bored as he was with hiding, and he jumped out, throwing debris all around. Using the train for cover, the yetis ran alongside, momentarily avoiding detection from the Greebos.

The cavern stretched for a long way into the mountain before it narrowed to the width of a mine shaft and twisted down into the ground. The railway track only stretched a short distance into the cavern, and the train was not going to stop.

"Over there!" shouted Albrecht, pointing to a large, cage-like elevator resting at the wall of the cavern. Chains on its top rose up through a shaft into the ceiling, heading into the unknown.

Suddenly a luminous green laser blast fizzed through the air above the yetis. They dived onto the floor, losing the train's protection. Saar rolled over and picked himself up as another shot winged its way through the air. He spotted the armed Greebo in the distance. Its eyes were flashing red.

"We've got trouble!" he announced.

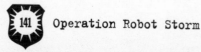

THE MYTHICAL 9TH DIVISION 141 Operation Robot Storm

All the Greebos stopped working, and the blue lights of their eyes started to flash red. They raised their pickaxes into the air and ran at the yetis

"Run!" shouted Albrecht.

As deadly green laser beams flashed around the cavern, the yetis charged to the elevator. Albrecht reached it first and un-latched the door. He jumped in through its narrow entrance, followed by Saar, who hit a lever outside with the end of his staff. Timonen reached them just as the elevator jolted into action. He attempted to squeeze in, but he couldn't fit through. A bright green energy ray hit the wall beside him, and a ripple of luminous light coursed outwards through the rock.

"Rotten yaks' teeth!" snarled Timonen.

He slammed the door shut and charged back into the cavern as the elevator shuddered upwards.

"Timonen!" yelled Albrecht, as the train overpowered the buffers and careened into the cavern wall. "What are you doing?!"

Chapter 10: Going Up!

THUMP!

HURRY UP!

GRRRRR.

145

With the ding of a bell, the elevator slowed to a halt, and the door swung open. Albrecht and Saar were in a small, shiny room, with polished metal walls that looked as if they'd been buffed to death. There was a glass door at the far end, and for the time being, the coast was clear.

"Hurry up!" said Timonen.

The two yetis stepped into the room and lifted up the cage – a few inches was all they could manage with the weight of Timonen hanging from the bottom. He gripped the edge of the floor with his free hand and pushed upwards with his shoulders, wedging his body between the elevator and the floor so he could pull himself up fully. With a grunt and a growl, he squeezed himself into the room.

"Greebo decontamination. Greebo decontamination," announced a speaker overhead.

A metal wall slid down in front of the elevator, trapping the yetis in the room. Next, a scalding shower of hot water rained down from the roof. The water eased, and then gloopy soap drizzled down onto the yetis. They looked at each other, knowing what was to come. Once again the hot water gushed down onto their heads, forming a dense froth over their fur, which ran down into gutters on the floor. When the yetis were free of soap, the water stopped, and a torrent of warm air blasted through the room, drying them off. They looked as though they'd just walked out of the hairdressers'.

Saar walked up to Timonen and sniffed him.

"You've never smelled so clean," he said.

Timonen sniffed his armpits.

"Lavender?" he said. "I smell like an old granny!"

"Greebo decontamination complete. Greebo decontamination complete," announced the speaker.

The doors to the room slid open, and they walked out into a frozen hallway. The floor was like a mirror, and opaque glass doors lined the walls, revealing only blurred images of what was behind.

Suddenly the yetis were blasted by an alarm siren screaming in the distance, and a blue light on the ceiling began to flash. A cold shiver ran down Albrecht's back.

"I guess everyone knows we're here," he said. "It's time to find Balaclava."

"Let me at 'em," said Timonen, who was spoiling for a fight. "I'm not scared of robots!"

Saar walked to one of the doors and tried opening it. There were no handles or buttons to press. He gazed through the glass, trying to get an idea of what was behind it.

"It's a big blur," said Saar.

Timonen strode over and gripped the edges of the door with his fingertips.

"Stop!" yelled Albrecht. "Wait!"

 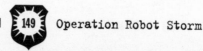

It was too late. The panel of glass was high above Timonen's head, and a troop of Greebos was staring at them from within the room. Each held a very menacing laser gun.

"Intruders!" said the Greebos in unison.

The yetis looked at each other as the flashing blue light turned to red.

"Run!" yelled Albrecht.

They hurtled along the corridor, slipping and sliding on the ice and bumping off the walls like a trio of pinballs.

"If there's trouble to be found, you'll find it!" shouted Saar breathlessly, trying to be heard above the siren.

"Don't you shout at me!" the big yeti bellowed back.

They followed a turn in the corridor and ran straight into a much larger glass door. It was taller than Timonen and wider than him too. Albrecht's eyes were rammed right up to the glass, but he couldn't see through. Whatever was inside was shrouded in darkness. The noise of the chasing Greebos was growing louder all the time. Suddenly three bolts of green light hit the icy wall to the yetis' side, and a sizzling wisp of steam drifted into the air.

"Break the door down!" ordered Albrecht.

Timonen looked at him angrily.

"What, and get the blame for whatever we find inside?" he replied. "Oh, no, not this time."

Saar held his staff up to Timonen's nose.

"If you don't do this," he said, as another laser beam hit the wall next to them, "I'm going lose my temper."

"Scare me some more, why don't you!" said Timonen, crossing his arms.

Saar breathed in, filling out his chest.

The last thing Albrecht wanted was for Saar to get angry. Saar *never* got angry. He gripped the side of his backpack, and the Sonic Flare dropped into his hand.

"If you want something done properly," he muttered, stabbing the device into the glass, "do it yourself."

The Flare's pointed end buzzed and glowed a bright orange, turning yellow then white as it warmed to melting point. Albrecht clicked a button on its side, and the door started to vibrate. With an ear-piercing squeal it shattered into a thousand tiny fragments.

"Now stop arguing and run!" he ordered.

The yetis charged on into a dark corridor. A few dotted lights lit up the edges of the walls like a runway, leading far into the distance. Albrecht glanced behind him and noticed that the Greebos had caught up with them, but they'd stopped running. Instead they were blocking the path and cutting off their retreat.

"Keep running," said Albrecht confidently, pounding further down the corridor.

A set of metal doors came into view at the end of the corridor. The yetis stopped, but the doors opened of their own accord. Albrecht started to choke. They'd found the entrance to an enormous workshop, lit by thousands and thousands of bright fluorescent bulbs. Machines growled and clanked as cartloads of minerals were worked into Greebo body parts. Conveyor belts moved back and forth on raised production lines, carrying thousands and thousands of unfinished Greebos. On the floor, thousands and thousands of complete and very much working Greebos were lined up ready for action. And there were thousands and thousands of laser guns in their hands.

Albrecht clutched his head and nearly tore his fur out.

"A Greebo factory," he said. "Of all the lousy luck!"

Four Greebos dropped down from above and landed right in front of the yetis. They were of the large variety, the Greebo 2000s, and their lasers were aimed right at the Mythical 9th.

"Intruders intercepted," announced one of the Greebos.

Suddenly the whole factory was filled with the voice of Balaclava, his words springing from speakers on every robot.

"Excellent!" said the evil genius. "Bring them to me!"

The yetis were whisked away along the corridor, back the way they'd come.

"Do not attempt escape," said a Greebo.

Albrecht looked around at the crowd of robots following them, each armed with a laser gun. He wasn't even going to try. They were marched into a large glass elevator, and with the Greebo guards squeezed in around them, they moved upwards. The elevator rose slowly, passing floor after floor until it slowed and stopped. The doors slid open, and the yetis were forced out into Balaclava's control room. The evil mastermind was standing with his hands behind his back, waiting for them.

"Come in! Come in!" he said. "And you can drop your weapons and luggage, thank you!"

Albrecht looked at his friends, then removed his backpack while Saar reluctantly lowered his staff to the floor.

"Goooood!" said Balaclava, walking closer, looking the yetis up and down in wonder.

"You really are amazing," he said. "Quite unlike anything I've ever seen before."

He tried to touch Timonen's fur, but the yeti batted away his hand. The Greebos snapped to attention and rammed their laser guns into his back.

"Oh, now, come on," said Balaclava. "I wouldn't want us to get off to a bad start!"

He turned around and walked to his control panel. With a press of a button, the screens flickered and tuned in to images of London. The city was under siege from ice and snow.

"What have you done?" said Albrecht, in shock.

"What? Don't you like my work?!" taunted Balaclava.

Albrecht shook his head in annoyance. Balaclava looked up at the screens, and his eyes lit up.

"I decided to freeze London first," he said, "to check that the Elemental is fully operational."

"The what?" said Saar.

"The Elemental," replied Balaclava. "My weather machine."

"But how can a machine control the weather?" asked Albrecht.

"Because I made it, and I'm a genius!"

"You may be a genius," said Timonen, "but you look ridiculous. Even Saar has better dress sense."

"Do not upset me," said Balaclava angrily. "Remember that I have your little friend as hostage."

"Gruff?" said Albrecht. "What have you done with him?"

"Oh, nothing much," said Balaclava breezily. "He's just feeling a little … frosty."

Saar growled under his breath. Despite his better instincts, his anger level was rising.

"But less of my prisoner," said Balaclava. "I want to know more about you!"

The yetis remained silent.

"You work for the British Army, then?"

Balaclava signaled to one of his robots, and it dragged away Albrecht's backpack and Saar's staff. When he got no reply from the yetis, he carried on.

"I'll soon find out anyway," he said. "Your mission has failed. If the British government thinks you are its saviors, then they've got an icy shock coming."

"What are you going to do?" said Albrecht.

Balaclava laughed.

"Assuming I'm not going to get my trillion dollars, then I'll freeze Washington. And then I'll set my sights on Beijing, then Paris, then Moscow."

"Moscow is already icy," said Albrecht. "I've been there, I know."

"Then I'm sure there are many other countries to freeze instead."

"Why are you doing this?" said Saar.

"Have you still not figured it out?" said Balaclava. "I want to be rich. Filthy, stinking rich! What couldn't I do with a

 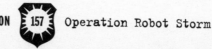

trillion dollars? And even if I don't get it, my weather machine will soon ensure that I rule the world anyway. There's no way I can fail!"

The evil genius walked back to his control panel and pressed a blue button. A *clunk-click* noise came from the wall beside the TV screens, and a glass drawer slid out into the room. Balaclava bent down and withdrew a large laser gun with a metallic sphere secured to its top.

"This, my furry friends, is what I call my Thermogun."

He gripped a knob on the gun's side, which helpfully had the word HOT engraved on one side and FROSTY on the other. As he twisted it towards FROSTY, the sphere jerked slightly, then started to spin. Thin veins of glowing energy crisscrossed its surface. The yetis shrank back, only to find the Greebos' laser guns forcing them forward.

"Don't worry," said Balaclava. "This won't hurt … much."

Chapter 11: Cold Feet

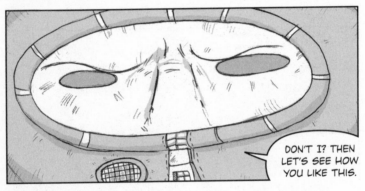

160

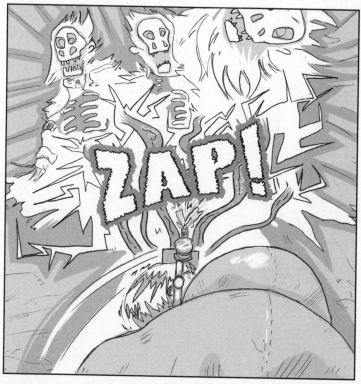

GREEBOS, TAKE THEM AWAY. I'LL QUESTION THEM LATER.

The robots wrestled the ice-bound yetis onto three enormous carts and rolled them into the elevator. The doors closed, and a Greebo pressed a button to make the elevator go down.

"Exit level, please!" said Timonen, tapping the robot on the shoulder. "Always ask your guests first."

"He's getting no tip from me," said Albrecht.

"Just you wait," said Timonen. "When the time comes, I'll give him the biggest tip he's ever had."

"Greebos do not require tips," said the Greebo.

"Typical," said Albrecht. "No sense of humor."

After plunging deep below ground, the robots wheeled them out of the elevator and down into the mines through a series of heavy iron doors.

"Watch it!" said Timonen, wobbling, as they were bumped back and forth.

The Greebos didn't reply. Instead, they tipped the yetis off the carts and dragged them into a dimly-lit tunnel. Then the robots marched away, bolting the doors behind them.

"Brilliant," said Albrecht, lying awkwardly on the floor.

He raised his iced legs and dropped them forcefully on the ground. Apart from scratches, the block suffered little damage.

When he looked up, he saw two giant ice cubes a little way down the tunnel.

"Gruff?!" he exclaimed.

The boy was frozen solid inside a block of ice, with an angry look on his face. In the small cube next to him was a mountain sheep.

"And a baby yak!" said Timonen, disgusted. "How dare they?"

Saar dragged himself across the floor and placed his hand on the ice surrounding the boy. For a few seconds he remained quiet.

"His heart is still beating," said Saar.

The other yetis breathed out with relief.

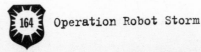

"Same as the soldiers out on the glacier," Saar added. "With this kind of power, Balaclava could be unstoppable."

Timonen picked at the ice on his legs, but even his robust nails couldn't cut into it.

"We have to do something!" said Albrecht, tiring of feeling so useless.

"By the time this ice melts around our legs – if it ever melts – the world will be finished," said Saar.

Timonen slammed his fists into the ice block, but only succeeded in hurting his hands.

"We need some heat," said Albrecht.

He let his head fall backwards onto the rocky wall. He relaxed, and as he shut his eyes, he suddenly felt an irregular vibration within the rock. He sat quietly for a second, waiting to make sure of it.

"Can you hear something?" he asked.

The others looked at him blankly.

"Touch the wall…"

The others put their hands against the rock and soon felt the vibration within.

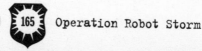

"Weird," said Saar.

The vibration grew stronger, until it became a loud rumble within the wall.

"Sounds like a drill," said Albrecht.

"Miners?" said Saar.

The yetis looked at each other.

The wall was visibly shaking now, and the yetis toppled into the tunnel and dragged themselves as far away as possible. The rumbling grew louder and louder, until a fine spray of grit and rock spluttered to the ground. Clumps of stone tumbled down, and finally a large rock drill appeared through a hole, breaking apart the wall with ease. Beams of white light entered the tunnel, and as the drill grumbled to a halt, a miner pushed through.

"Now there's a bit of luck!" he announced, his face covered in dust. "Ang! Boys! Look what we found!"

"Ang!" said Albrecht.

"Yetis?" said Ang, squeezing through the hole. "Have you seen Gruff?"

Albrecht pointed to the giant ice cube.

"Oh, no..." said Ang. "Is he alive? Why does he never listen?"

She rushed to Gruff and clutched the ice with her gloved hands.

"He's still alive," said Saar. "But he needs defrosting without delay."

One by one, Gruff's family and friends entered the mine shaft. Most of them held laser guns – the sort normally carried by Greebo 2000s. The miners' faces were ecstatic, until they saw the boy trapped within a block of ice.

"Get the drill on him!" said Ang. "Be careful, mind."

Saar raised his hands.

"Maybe try it on one of us first," he said. "Just to be on the safe side."

"Yeah!" said Timonen. "Try it on me. Drill away!"

The miner with the drill looked to Ang, who shrugged and agreed.

"Right you are, then," said the miner.

Timonen watched as the drill revved up and ripped into the ice block around his legs. Chips of ice sprayed everywhere, but it was effective, and the drill had soon cleaved the block in two.

With a little more expert drilling the blocks had disintegrated, and Timonen could stand up.

"Right," said Albrecht. "Me next!"

The miner drilled through the yetis' icy bonds, and when they were all done, he turned to Gruff.

"I've got to try," he said. "At least get a bit of the ice off him?"

Everyone agreed that he had to do something, so he started up the motor and set to work carving Gruff out of his block of

ice. Like a master sculptor with a block of marble, the miner followed the shape of Gruff's body until the block was almost human-shaped.

"How heavy is he?" asked Ang. "Can we carry him back like that?"

Two miners picked up the frozen boy and nodded their heads.

"Hey!" said Timonen, interrupting. "Do the yak too!"

The miners looked confused, but they weren't going to argue with him. They cut away most of the ice from the sheep and promised to thaw it properly.

"So how did you find us?" said Albrecht.

"After Gruff disappeared," said Ang, "those robots attacked us, but we got the better of them. We stole two of their snow-mobiles to get through the storm and then followed some old mine maps to get in. Mountain people know their mountains..."

"Well," said Albrecht, "for a second time you've saved us."

"Don't mention it," said Ang. "But you have this situation sorted out now, right? I need to look after my son... And once he's defrosted, tell him off!"

"We know what we have to do," said Albrecht.

Timonen slammed his fists together. He was ready for the fight.

"Take these lasers," said Ang.

Timonen grabbed one of the guns, but his finger wouldn't fit through the trigger. He snorted in disgust.

"You're better off without one, anyway," said Albrecht, taking it from him.

"Wouldn't want you shooting us," added Saar, as he was handed his own.

"Right," said Ang, stepping back through the wall. "Good luck."

"Thanks," said Albrecht.

He shook down his shoulders and readied the laser gun in his hands.

"Mythical 9th Division," he said. "It's time to save the world."

THE MYTHICAL **9th** DIVISION

Chapter 12: The Elemental

"**S**tay down there!" Albrecht ordered Timonen. "Give us cover!"

Timonen threw his clenched fist in the air in response and turned to smash another wave of Greebos into the tunnel walls. Saar and Albrecht raced on, coming to a halt in a gigantic blackened hall with a shining metallic furnace built at one end. Conveyor belts crisscrossed the hall, dragging lumps of coal to the furnace. A team of Greebos was hard at work shoveling the fuel into the flames. As the yetis stopped their charge, the Greebos turned to look at them.

A chorus of "Intruders!" crackled through their mouths.

"This way!" said Albrecht.

In the far corner of the hall, bolted to the wall, was a ladder which rose up into the ceiling.

"Up! We've got to go up to reach the Elemental!"

The Greebos seemed torn between filling the furnace and stopping the yetis, and Albrecht used this to his advantage. He leapt from one conveyor belt to the next, using their forward movement to build up speed. Saar followed his every jump, and soon they'd reached the far end. The Greebos charged at them as they were climbing the ladder, but with only shovels for weapons they could do little to stop them.

Albrecht climbed up through the ceiling and found himself in another cavernous room filled with machinery. Huge upright spinning discs, spaced at even intervals over the length of the room, whirred loudly.

"It's a power turbine," said Saar, clambering through the hole in the floor. "We're in a power station!"

He aimed his laser gun at the top of the ladder and blasted it from the wall, sending Greebos toppling down to the floor below. Albrecht looked over the machine and followed its numerous pipes and cables to a metal box attached to the wall. There was a screen on its front, and glowing bars of light flickered and dipped depending on the level of electricity being created. He read the small digital display.

 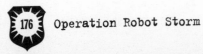

"There's enough power coming through here to fuel a city," said Albrecht.

"And look!" said Saar.

Through a glass door at the far end he could see a tremendous blue light.

"The Elemental?" said Albrecht.

He walked closer and pressed his nose to the glass. Through the flickering blue light he could see the room was circular. Albrecht focused on the source of light: Streaks of blue lightning were coursing around a huge metal ball in the center of the room. It was spinning, suspended between the roof and floor by two pyramids, one above, one below. Traveling around its top was a scaffold walkway, which was securely bolted to the wall.

"Greebos everywhere," said Albrecht, watching the robots pace along the walkway to a control room perched high on the wall.

Suddenly the walls around them started to shake.

"Another earthquake?" said Saar, stumbling from left to right.

"You know what that means!" said Albrecht.

*　*　*

"Prisoners escaped. Prisoners in engine room," said a Greebo 2000.

Balaclava marched around his room in a fury.

"How could they have escaped?" he shouted.

The Greebo didn't answer.

"Robots…" muttered Balaclava. "Useless robots." He paused to watch the two yetis on the wall of screens in front of him. They were going to disable the Elemental! He had to stop them!

He walked to his ice chair, sat down and took a deep breath. He knew it was risky to use the Elemental again so soon, but the yetis had forced him to act.

He pulled a lever on the control panel, and the room shook as the Elemental powered up.

The Greebo tapped a button on its neck, and a beep sounded from its speaker.

"Soldiers surrounding storm barrier," it said.

"Soldiers?" said Balaclava.

"Hundreds," said the Greebo.

Balaclava sank into his chair and pushed the little zipper of his jacket right up to his nose.

 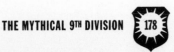

"They're not ready," he muttered to himself. "Not ready…"

Balaclava slammed his fist into the desk.

"It's time to get serious."

"Awaiting orders," said the Greebo.

"The Greebo 3000s," said Balaclava. "The programming is still a bit ragged, but I have no choice. Send the Greebo 3000s to find those yetis. Then send all other Greebos to intercept the soldiers. The Elemental is about to be pushed further than ever before."

The Greebo marched away, and Balaclava pulled himself from his chair. He breathed deeply, rolled his shoulders and readied himself for television. With the flick of a switch, the displays changed to the view of his control room.

"World!" he announced, walking onto the screens. "London knows what it is like to suffer, and the chill has swept across all of Britain."

Balaclava lifted his hands to his chest and rubbed them against each other.

"So now it is time for America to feel the wrath of the Elemental."

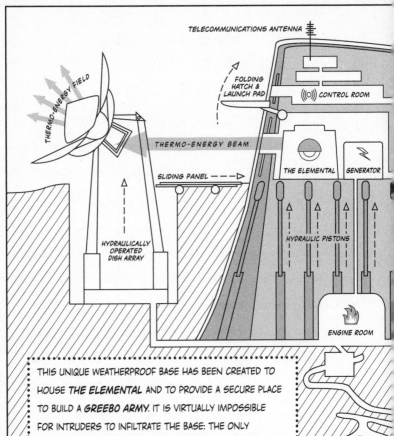

TELECOMMUNICATIONS ANTENNA

THERMO-ENERGY FIELD

FOLDING HATCH & LAUNCH PAD

(((o))) CONTROL ROOM

THERMO-ENERGY BEAM

SLIDING PANEL - - - ▷

THE ELEMENTAL

GENERATOR

HYDRAULICALLY OPERATED DISH ARRAY

HYDRAULIC PISTONS

ENGINE ROOM

THIS UNIQUE WEATHERPROOF BASE HAS BEEN CREATED TO HOUSE **THE ELEMENTAL** AND TO PROVIDE A SECURE PLACE TO BUILD A **GREEBO ARMY**. IT IS VIRTUALLY IMPOSSIBLE FOR INTRUDERS TO INFILTRATE THE BASE: THE ONLY WEAK SPOTS ARE THE OLD MINING TUNNELS. SHOULD ANY SECURITY BREACH OCCUR HERE, GREEBOS WILL BE ON GUARD TO PREVENT ANY INCIDENT FROM ESCALATING.

THE MYTHICAL **9th** DIVISION

ITEM: BALACLAVA'S SECRET BAS
STATUS: *TOP-SECRET*

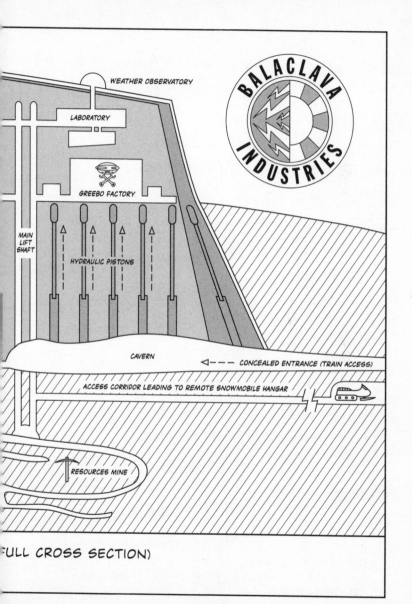

Albrecht twisted the heavy, wheel-like handle that wouldn't have been out of place on a submarine. The lock finally opened, and the door squealed as it swung inwards. The floor sloped down to the spherical Elemental machine, which was whirling around faster and faster, sending a powerful wind coursing around the room. Albrecht felt his hair rise as he walked in. He turned to Saar and found he looked more like a pompom than a yeti.

"Static!" shouted Saar, raising his voice over the crackling energy of the weather machine. "We look ridiculous!"

Albrecht gripped his laser gun, which was becoming lost in his fluffy fur.

"How are we going to get up there?" said Albrecht, wriggling his toes and looking at the walkway where the few Greebos were busy pressing buttons and pulling levers.

"I don't think we need to worry about that," said Saar, as the two yetis started to float in the strange invisible energy field that surrounded the machine. Unable to stop themselves, they rose into the air and were soon spinning around the huge metal ball, with flashes of electricity zipping around them.

"I feeeel siiiiicccck!" wailed Albrecht, flying around the room like a hairy balloon.

Saar, of course, was quite at home with the sensation.

Just then the Greebos on the walkways stopped moving. Their eyes turned from blue to red as their programming responded to new orders. Alarm lights flashed in the control room at the end of the walkway, and the Greebos finally caught sight of the two yetis spinning around in the pull of the Elemental. With their magnetic feet secured to the walkways, the robots could get close to the great ball of energy without being affected by its pull. But there was nothing they could do to retrieve the yetis.

Whilst Albrecht felt ill from his constant spinning, Saar had focused his mind and was watching the Greebos with each pass of the walkway. His hair was still floating around him, and his scarf was snapping in his wake, but his eyes were very much under control.

"They can't touch us," he said to himself, as he circled the Elemental. "Why is that?"

He turned his attention to the ball of energy in the center of the room. It was spinning faster and faster as it powered up, and the sparks of blue energy fizzed around it with greater ferocity than ever before.

Suddenly, the metal ball split horizontally along its center, and its parts drifted away from each other to reveal a white-hot, blazing core. Electrical sparks shot out into the room, and Saar looked at his hands to see that his laser gun was glowing. He saw Albrecht spinning uncontrollably beside him and noticed his was doing the same.

A bolt of lightning leapt out of the metallic ball and crashed into Saar's laser gun. He could do nothing to stop the overpowering pull from dragging the gun into the white core. Another bolt sizzled out and tore Albrecht's laser from his hands, and it too went spiraling into the white ball of energy. The outlines of the weapons were visible for mere seconds before they vanished into nothing. Saar grew worried. He looked around the room and realized that the Greebos had started to glow too. The Elemental was malfunctioning.

"An unworldly magnetic force," he said. "Like the poles of

the Earth, this machine is pure magnetic energy! And it's going into overdrive!"

Saar realized it was very bad news indeed. One by one the Greebos were plucked from their walkway and sucked headfirst into the Elemental. They vaporized immediately. Magnetic power and metal clearly weren't good for each other.

Timonen took a breather from all the robot pummeling he'd been doing to check on the whereabouts of his friends. Greebos attempted to cling onto his long fur, punching his kneecaps, but he took it all very well. With a flick and a swat, most of them were dispatched into the rocky walls.

"Albrecht?!" he shouted, his voice traveling down through the mine shafts in echoes. "Saar?!"

He reached the engine room that the yetis had headed into just a few minutes earlier and saw two Greebos squashed under a fallen metal ladder. He leapt across the conveyor belts and peered up into the hole in the roof. There was no way he could get up there, and even if he could, he'd never squeeze through the gap.

"Right, then," he said, cracking his enormous knuckles. "Only one thing for it!"

He walked back the way he'd come, returning to the tunnel. A new wave of Greebos had arrived, their red eyes shining brightly. Timonen dipped his shoulder and charged into them like a bulldozer.

Balaclava reached forward and pressed the large red button, the one surrounded by black-and-yellow warning stripes.

"This is for you, Washington," he said.

The control panel's warning light shot on. The displays in front of him turned black, and the word ERROR flashed across the screens.

"Greebo 2000!" he shouted, pressing buttons and turning dials one after the other to try and put the matter right. Nothing worked.

The Greebo appeared.

"Something is very wrong," said Balaclava. "Prepare the snowcraft for immediate escape."

"Yes, sir," said the Greebo.

 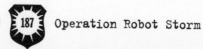

"And the Greebo 3000s?" asked Balaclava.

"Greebo 3000s on task."

"Excellent," said Balaclava.

He rushed to claim his Thermogun and stopped to stare at the control panel, which was displaying even more warning lights.

"Those yetis will never leave here alive," he said evilly.

The white core at the center of the Elemental started to pulsate and vibrate manically. Something new was happening. As the two metallic halves of the machine closed up to seal the burning energy at its heart, part of the outer wall of the room opened to show daylight. In the distance, out on the mountain, Saar spotted the immense satellite dish, unfurled and ready for action. Then, without so much as a pop, the metallic ball stopped turning. The yetis fell to the floor with a heavy thud.

Albrecht was desperately short of breath, and his head was spinning, just as his body had been only moments ago.

"At least my fur's back to normal," he muttered.

Saar picked up his friend and turned around to see the metal ball of the Elemental twist and buckle. Dents were forming on its surface, as though the massive ball of energy – which should have blasted through the window and traveled to the skies above Washington – was imploding.

"Where are our lasers?" whispered Albrecht, attempting to stand upright on his own.

"Inside that metal ball," said Saar, "along with the Greebos, which might be why it looks as though it's about to blow up."

Albrecht took a deep breath.

"Can you run?" asked Saar.

Albrecht nodded.

"Then I think it might be best if we did just that!"

The two yetis sprinted with every bit of energy they had towards the opening at the end of the room. They launched themselves out into the fresh air and went flying down the outside wall, tumbling down towards the mountain. As they hit the ground, a huge explosion ripped through the side of the secret hide-out, and a bright-blue light blasted into the sky.

Albrecht pulled himself to his feet and looked back up at

 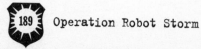

the towering building. It was missing half of its side, and smoke was billowing out into the air, but it was still standing. Greebos were crawling over it like ants.

"Timonen!" said Albrecht. "He's still in there!"

The hide-out lurched ominously to one side.

"It's Balaclava we need to find," said Saar. "Timonen can look after himself."

Albrecht rolled his shoulders.

"You're right. I only hope he's used his brain to get out of there."

Saar tightened the scarf around his neck.

"I'm not even going to reply to that," he said.

THE MYTHICAL 9th DIVISION

Chapter 13: The Greebo 3000s

192

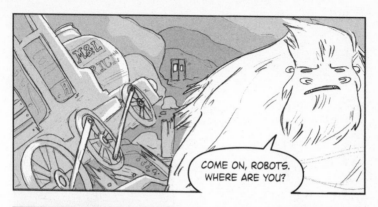

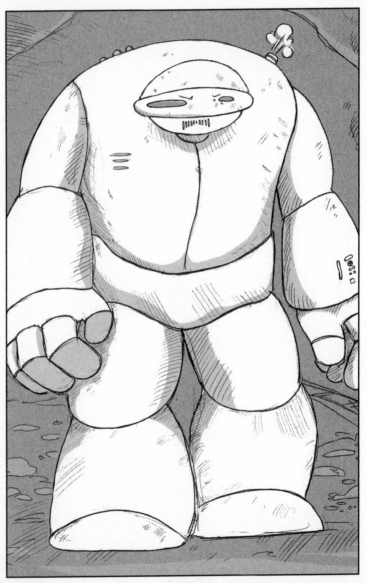

HALT!!
DO NOT ATTEMPT
TO MOVE!

Timonen dived through the air and hit the Greebo 3000 in the chest. The two giants grappled as they tumbled backwards through the tunnel and out into the daylight. The Greebo found its footing first, twisted over and threw Timonen away across the mountain. The yeti had never been thrown before. Once he'd skidded to a halt in the snow, he stood up and roared his indignation aloud, puffing out his chest so that it swelled to the size of a small car.

"How dare you..." he growled.

The Greebo stood tall and held out its right arm as if to shake a hand. Timonen marched towards it and then noticed that its right hand had been replaced with a laser gun. As four bright green beams shot towards the yeti, he jumped for cover, rolling through the snow before springing up onto his feet.

The huge Greebo ran at its target, spurts of steam blasting

from its joints. Its bright eyes never lost sight of Timonen, but the yeti knew better than to stand still. He leapt up the mountainside, clawing his way over the rocks and scree. Balaclava's hide-out was only a short distance from him, standing out like a jewel on the mountain. A plume of smoke was rising from its far side. Timonen craned his neck around and spotted the robot struggling to run on the rough ground; real feet were often better than flat metal feet.

"Smoke means trouble," said Timonen breathlessly, outrunning the Greebo. "And trouble means yetis."

The robot stopped running and resorted to his laser once more, placing a few choice shots up the mountain which sent snow and rocks down onto the yeti. Timonen shielded himself with his shoulder and then picked up a dislodged boulder. He held it high above his head and hurled it into the path of the Greebo. The laser in its arm blew the boulder to smithereens, and Timonen huffed as he tried to catch his breath. This Greebo was almost too good for him.

Albrecht and Saar ran around the base of the hide-out, looking for a way back in. The massive storm front that had protected

 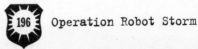

Balaclava's lair was thinning. With the Elemental destroyed, the evil mastermind no longer had any cover.

"There!" said Saar, spotting movement on a platform that stretched out over the side of the building like a helipad.

"If only I had my binoculars," said Albrecht angrily.

Saar began scaling the building's slippery surface.

"No time to worry about that now," he said, "just climb."

It was no different than navigating a glacier, and the yetis made light work of the climb. With a final effort they pulled themselves up onto the platform.

"Oh," said Saar.

Two teardrop-shaped snowcraft were lined up before them. They looked like spaceships, but built for icy, earth-bound conditions: Their sleek cabins rested on three skis, and large propellers were attached to their backs to power them over the snow.

And the yetis weren't alone.

"You!" screamed Balaclava, gesturing wildly with his Thermogun. He was guarded by two Greebos, one of them the huge kind that Timonen had encountered.

 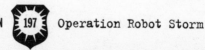

"Greebo 3000," snapped Balaclava, "get them!"

The yetis stood in awe of the giant robot as it thundered across the platform towards Saar. Balaclava and the other Greebo climbed into one of the snowcraft and switched on its engine.

"Albrecht," said Saar confidently, "I'll handle this. You go after them…"

Albrecht shot him a confused glance, but he wasn't going to question his friend's intentions. He ran to the second craft and pulled himself into the cabin only to be confronted by a control stick and a dashboard full of dials and buttons.

How on earth did the snowmobile start?

Saar dodged the first charge of the robot by sliding to the ground, but he had only a fraction of a second before the robot charged again. It smashed its huge fist into the floor as Saar rolled through its legs and jumped to his feet on the other side. The robot lurched over, its hand disappeared, and the gun slid into place at the end of its arm. With a bright green flash, its laser beam tore into the ground to the right of the yeti.

Saar dashed for cover, throwing himself through an open

door in the wall. When he looked up, he found himself in the center of Balaclava's control room. The displays were fuzzy or dead, and red lights were flashing all over. Laser beams suddenly coursed through the room, blowing the screens to pieces. The robot was intent on destruction. Saar ran along the corridor to the elevator, but the shaft was empty. There was no way down. There was no escape.

The Greebo 3000 appeared in the doorway, its laser gun throbbing with energy. It lifted its arm, and at that very moment, Saar heard Captain Ponkerton's muffled voice from behind him.

"Albrecht?! Come in, Albrecht!" he said.

"The RoAR!" cried Saar.

The Greebo fired, and Saar ducked. The wall exploded behind him, revealing a store of laser guns. On the floor was Albrecht's backpack, and standing next to it, was the Staff of Ages.

"No time to explain," shouted Saar into the air, as the Greebo fired again.

"Saar? Is that you?" said Ponkerton.

Saar swung the backpack onto his shoulders and took hold of his staff. He was feeling angrier than he had in years, and the robot was going to be very sorry.

With the staff pointed at the Greebo, Saar charged forward. As the robot fired, he pole-vaulted upwards and smashed his feet straight into its head. The Greebo toppled onto its back, and before it could make a move, Saar speared its face with the top of his staff. A bright electrical flash lit up the room, and a puff of smoke rose into the air. The robot shook a little, and then its arms clanged down onto the ground as its internal circuits closed down.

Saar withdrew his staff, cleaned the charred, smoke-stained end, and walked out of the control room into the sunlight.

Timonen was out of breath, but his luck was holding. He skated across a frozen lake, attempting to slide on his soles while dodging the laser blasts that were melting the ice below him. When he reached solid ground, he realized he could feel the heat of the sun. The storm was over. Traces of mist lingered in the distance, but there was very little sign that the storm barrier had ever been there.

Timonen noticed the Greebo stop and take stock of the situ-

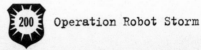

ation. Its massive metal head twisted to face the hide-out, and its hand touched its neck as if receiving orders. Without warning, it turned back to the yeti and let out a volley of laser blasts. Timonen ducked and dived, moving forward as much as he could to get out of the way of the deadly beams. Eventually he found a pile of rocks and darted behind them for cover.

"This isn't like you," he said angrily to himself. "Yetis don't hide!"

He breathed in, clenching his fists and shoring up every last morsel of power. He could hear the Greebo approaching, its laser beams hitting the rocks behind him with pinpoint accuracy. Timonen was ready.

He grabbed a rock in each hand and hurled them at the robot. As it blasted them out of the sky, Timonen charged, ramming his shoulder into its waist. The Greebo tumbled backwards, and Timonen grabbed its laser arm with both hands. He tightened his grip and twisted the metal of its joints until the gun was bent out of shape and facing upwards. The robot smacked Timonen to the floor and clambered to its feet, but its laser was useless. The Greebo tried to fire, but the laser shot back over its shoulder, searing into the mountain.

"See how you like this!" said Timonen, kicking out and knocking the robot to the ground.

He clutched the robot's huge leg and started to swing the Greebo around his body. The Greebo 3000 could do nothing as Timonen picked up speed and with a final deafening roar, flung him towards the mountain. The robot landed in a broken heap down on the glacier. Timonen sat down and breathed a sigh of relief. Steam rose from his fur, and snorts of hot air gushed from his nose.

He was contemplating how he'd almost met his match, when the noise of engines and propellers filled the air. Timonen looked up and saw white battle-helicopters powering down through the sky. Doors on their sides slid open, and long ropes flicked down to the ground. Timonen thought about running, but before he could move, hundreds of soldiers gracefully slid out and dropped down to the floor.

He jumped up, remembering that he was not to be seen by humans, when a soldier charged up to him.

"Hey, big guy!" shouted the soldier.

He was no ordinary military personnel. He was exceptionally tall, and his back was slightly hunched. His face was covered in a mask, and as well as the machine gun that was grasped in his big brown hairy hands, a sleek black backpack was strapped to his back. Long brown fur covered his body.

Timonen relaxed.

"Mythical 6th Division here to relieve you," he said. "Seems like you've had a few problems!"

"Thanks very much, Mr. Bigfoot," said Timonen. "But you're late as usual."

"We came as soon as we were asked. So where's this bad guy?"

Timonen pointed to the building.

"Up there somewhere," he said.

The bigfoot gave him a thumbs up and went running off towards the base.

"Oh!" said the bigfoot, pausing momentarily and turning back. "Hard luck in the Challenge! On home ground too…"

Timonen pretended not to hear.

———— 9th ————

Chapter 14: Back into the Wilderness

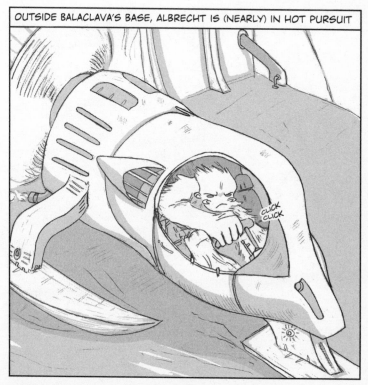

OUTSIDE BALACLAVA'S BASE, ALBRECHT IS (NEARLY) IN HOT PURSUIT

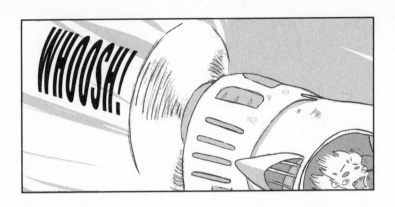

Albrecht soon had the hang of the snowcraft. It was fast and agile and made easy work of the dips and hollows of the ice sheet. He'd gotten within a hundred yards of Balaclava's craft, but the evil genius had a cold and calculating Greebo at the helm. The robot knew no fear and took more risks than Albrecht dared.

They navigated crevices and ravines, zooming through the thinnest of gaps with such precision that Albrecht never left the edge of his seat. There was no way he could relax: They were heading west, and Albrecht knew that only the sea lay that way.

"What are you playing at?" muttered Albrecht, swerving the craft to avoid a crack in the glacier. "Just where are you going?"

Balaclava leaned out of his craft and pointed the Thermo-gun at Albrecht. The evil genius had donned a pair of darkened goggles and was almost completely covered. He fired, and a frosty beam of bright-blue light whizzed past Albrecht's craft.

Balaclava took the gun inside, made a few adjustments to its settings, and leaned out again. He pulled its trigger once more, but this time aimed not at Albrecht, but at the ground in front of him.

The yeti steered the craft to the right, but as the Thermo-gun beam hit the ground, a mound of ice frosted up before him. The snowcraft tipped onto its side, still powering along at high speed, and shot up into the air. Albrecht pulled back on the control stick, but the craft was flying and twisting of its own accord. Balaclava fired again, but the beam missed and rock-eted up into the sky.

Albrecht held on for dear life as his snowcraft bounced back down onto the glacier, swerving wildly and gouging cuts into the ice with its skates. He looked up and suddenly realized there was nothing but horizon in the distance. The glacier seemed to come to an abrupt halt. But Balaclava wasn't stopping.

With an immense rush of panic, Albrecht pulled the control stick to the side and slammed his foot on the brake pedal. His craft skidded to one side and juddered as it scraped along the ice. Albrecht turned to face the horizon and watched as Balaclava's craft flew straight off the edge and disappeared.

With a screech and a howl, Albrecht's craft stopped dead,

 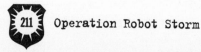

right at the edge of the glacier. He looked down from the cockpit and saw the crashing waves far below.

There was no way anyone could have survived the fall. The mission was over.

"Thank heavens you're alive!" said Captain Ponkerton. "I've had everyone – and I mean *everyone* – bothering me since you went missing."

Albrecht placed the RoAR on the dashboard of the snowcraft. The other yetis were sitting outside, and they were all hiding behind a wall of slowly melting ice.

"Well, Balaclava almost had the better of us," said Albrecht, "but he won't trouble us again."

"I should hope not!" said the Captain. "It's been a terrible few days, but those Greebo specifications you forwarded have proved indispensable! Not only did they include details of their programming, but there was also a schematic of Balaclava's hide-out. He'd managed to take over the rebuilding of the cafe at the top of the mountain without anyone knowing. But that's by the by. You've saved the day once again."

Albrecht rested back in the cockpit and relaxed.

"And the human contact?" he asked.

"We've sent operatives into the mines to discuss the issue. We've told them that if they keep quiet, we'll let them take the credit for disarming Balaclava. The papers are already excited about the prospect of it. 'Welsh heroes save the day!' and all that. They'll become stars in their own right."

"And Gruff?" asked Albrecht.

"He defrosted nicely," said Ponkerton. "We were concerned his brain might have gone a bit mushy, but his mother insists that's what he's always like."

"I feel that we owe him something," said Albrecht.

"I'll see to it that he gets an old, decommissioned RoAR," said Ponkerton. "We'll make sure it plays all the new games for him."

"And he won't talk?" said Albrecht.

"Not if his mother has anything to say about it," he replied.

"And how are the glaciers shaping up?" asked Albrecht.

"The temperature is increasing, slowly. London is struggling to come to terms with it – trains and buses aren't running, but then there's nothing new there. In a year or so, everything should be back to normal."

"Excellent," said Albrecht.

"And what about you three?" asked Ponkerton.

"I could do with a rest," said Albrecht.

Timonen and Saar echoed his comments.

"As things stand," said Ponkerton, "the Mythical 6th is running the cleanup operation. They overwhelmed the Greebo army, and they'll soon start work on dismantling the secret hide-out. You've more than earned some time off. Shall I send a pickup?"

"In a day or so," said Albrecht. "I'd like to do some sightseeing in this snowcraft I've picked up. I've become quite attached to it."

"Right you are," said Ponkerton. "Just let me know if you need anything."

"We won't need a thing," said Albrecht.

Ponkerton saluted and bid them farewell.

"Good job, boys, I knew you were the right team to call!"

The RoAR flickered off, and Albrecht breathed a long, drawn-out sigh.

"Fancy a spin?" he said.

Saar smiled and clambered into the snowcraft. Timonen had no choice but to climb on top.

"I always get the worst seat," he growled.

"If you could actually fit on a seat it would help," said Saar.

Albrecht pressed the ignition and clutched the controls.

"Everybody ready?" he said.

"Of course," said Timonen.

THE
END

THE MYTHICAL 9th DIVISION

Appendix: The Founding of the Mythical 9th Division

Much of the work of the Mythical 9th Division is shrouded in secrecy, but there are a few known facts.

The history of the Mythical 9th Division stretches back to the mid nineteenth century when the East India Trading Company attempted to survey and map the Himalayas (the Great Trigonometric Survey). The mission was fraught with political and geographical difficulties, so the British employed local help, training men from Indian border states to take measurements and chart terrain (these men were known as the Pundits). Because of their origin, the Pundits were able to cross northern borders where the British could not. Despite this, the missions were still carried out in the utmost secrecy for fear of execution or torture if they were found out.

THE FIRST HUMAN–YETI ENCOUNTER

It was on a survey mission in 1865 that the British Army

first discovered and worked with yetis.

It was on one of these surveying missions in 1865 that a Pundit first encountered a yeti, whose knowledge of the region was unmatched. With the aid of yeti help, the survey was a qualified success. A bond was then forged between the British Army and the yetis, which has continued through to the current day.

After the official formation of the United Nations in 1945, it was decided that all the mythical troops of the world should be ratified and united under one top-secret umbrella organization: L.E.G.E.N.D.S. (League of Extraordinary and Genetically ENhanced Defence Squads). There are eight other mythical divisions working alongside the yetis.

The Mythical 9th Division has always consisted of three yetis, a number considered incredibly lucky in Tibet. The three yetis that currently make up the team all have German code names, a remnant of the division's reconnaissance work during World War II when its current members, Saar, Timonen and Albrecht, first worked together.

Over the years, eight yetis have served in the Mythical 9th Division. They have worked in some of the world's most hostile environments, where ice and snow might hamper British efforts.

 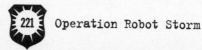

Their missions have always been top-secret, but rumors and conspiracy theories abound.

The first rumor surrounding the work of the division relates to Captain Scott and his quest to reach the South Pole. Certain government circles have suggested that Captain Scott refused yeti assistance in his doomed 1912 Antarctic expedition. His failure to utilize yeti knowledge, as well as his reluctance concerning the use of dogs, may well have contributed to his downfall.

Another controversial story linked to the Mythical 9th Division is that they may have shadowed Edmund Hillary in his successful ascent of Everest in 1953. The British government is thought to have been determined that a Commonwealth expedition should reach the summit first, particularly after the mourning and loss of George Mallory in 1924. There is no solid evidence to support this theory although, teasingly, Hillary and Tensing Norgay reported seeing large footprints on the mountain.

Other more substantial stories relate to the yetis' essential work during World War II. They are thought to have assisted the Norwegian Resistance in hindering Hitler's Atomic Energy Project in Telemark, and they may also have been on the Eastern Front during Operation Barbarossa, relaying intelligence to the Allies of the German whereabouts. Russian eyewitnesses report sightings of peculiarly hairy men walking without difficulty through the worst blizzards.

Whatever the rumors, it is clear the Mythical 9th Division continues to work tirelessly for British interests and the world.

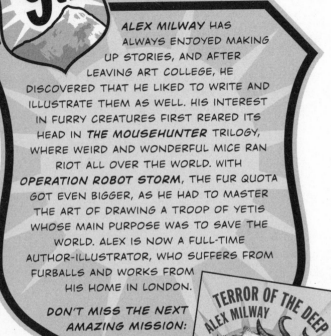

9th

ALEX MILWAY HAS ALWAYS ENJOYED MAKING UP STORIES, AND AFTER LEAVING ART COLLEGE, HE DISCOVERED THAT HE LIKED TO WRITE AND ILLUSTRATE THEM AS WELL. HIS INTEREST IN FURRY CREATURES FIRST REARED ITS HEAD IN *THE MOUSEHUNTER* TRILOGY, WHERE WEIRD AND WONDERFUL MICE RAN RIOT ALL OVER THE WORLD. WITH *OPERATION ROBOT STORM*, THE FUR QUOTA GOT EVEN BIGGER, AS HE HAD TO MASTER THE ART OF DRAWING A TROOP OF YETIS WHOSE MAIN PURPOSE WAS TO SAVE THE WORLD. ALEX IS NOW A FULL-TIME AUTHOR-ILLUSTRATOR, WHO SUFFERS FROM FURBALLS AND WORKS FROM HIS HOME IN LONDON.

DON'T MISS THE NEXT AMAZING MISSION:

TERROR OF THE DEEP
ALEX MILWAY

MYTHICAL **9** DIVISION

Armed, dangerous and covered in fur!